SATISFACTION

Other Books by Sid Huston

BASK: Real Spirituality

BASK: Sexual Freedom and Sexual Restraint

BASK: Satisfaction

BASK: Wisdom

BASK

Satisfaction

Alive, Rich, and Free

Sid Huston

Dedication

I dedicate this book to my children and grandchildren and their generation. My hope is that they will enjoy beautiful relationships and live satisfied and at peace with God. I desire that they delight in God, for I know that when they do, they will be surrounded by goodness and mercy and they will live in the house of the LORD forever. They will forever be satisfied (adapted from Psalm 23).

Table of Contents

Preface

In the first book in this BASK series of Christian fiction, *Real Spirituality*, we show how our flesh functions like a pirate. In the book, we explain how rejection inflames our flesh and gets us to hack and slash and chase like a pirate. After reading this treatise, it is easy to see why pirates don't have good relationships. What followed were *Sexual Freedom and Sexual Restraint*. Pirates chased after sex for all the wrong reasons. The craving for sexual fulfillment is strong, and pirates are known to "howl at the moon" as they chase this experience. In this book—to the readers' surprise—we discovered that God made sex to be enjoyed and demonstrated how to have true satisfaction in life.

In the first book, we told the story about Captain Henry Morgan, the real swashbuckler who made hundreds of pirates rich by his exploits and the capturing of much booty. He also turned Port Royal, Jamaica, into a pirate haven with a smorgasbord of pleasures for every pirate's delights. This port was made for pirate ships and protected by pirates. He made sure there were plenty of prostitutes in the whorehouses and lots of rum in the taverns. It was regarded as the most wicked place in the world.

In this book and in this context, we come to find satisfaction in very unusual place. Captain Morgan's flagship was called the *Satisfaction*. And he sacrificed it to save his own skin; it is a heck of a story. But, in this book, *Satisfaction*, a love story ensues, and some colorful characters emerge. Tim and Esther find each other in a garden just above Port Royal. They begin a beautiful and life-giving relationship in spite of an array of dramatic differences. With the help of Esther's Papa Peter, the couple develops a wonderful relationship. There are tremendous lessons to be learned, but, best of all, they begin to experience true satisfaction. If you long to be satisfied, you will enjoy this voyage. Sail on!

Acknowledgments

No man is an island. And those of you who know me know that my wealth is in my friends. I also want to make my friends rich, with *true* riches.

This BASK series of historical Christian fiction only came about because God blessed me with friends who have extraordinary talents. Truly the following are ordinary people who have let God pour in to their lives some special abilities. And—like Tom Sawyer—I haven't failed to use my friends.

Terrie Solheim has been heaven-sent. Her editing skills are excellent. She has made many great "edits" and offered me some valuable suggestions. Her heart for God and God's Word has made her a valuable editor.

Missy Call is a longtime friend who loves to connect people through social media. Those of you who will interact with us through Facebook, Instagram, and our BASK.Love website will get to know Missy and appreciate her as I do. If you have a prayer request or a question, she will engage you promptly.

She will make sure you have regular encouragement through our pirate attitudes blog site and YouTube videos. (This is the blog that will flog your flesh.)

David Wolf is a recent friend who has done an outstanding job producing our *Real Spirituality* audio book. When you listen to these books, you will appreciate David's professionalism and commitment to excellence.

Chris Braden and his Sport of Marketing, and Roger Brinkley, have inspired me with many spiritual insights and applications. Our regular barbeque lunches have been laced with many "ahoy" moments for me. My wealth is in my friends, and these dear brothers are a treasure trove of business and relationship insights.

I owe many thanks to Michelle Vandepas and Camille Truman. Michelle has tremendous know-how about publishing and has brought these books to life. And Camille has done a beautiful job with the layout and cover design.

This team has helped me put together a series of Christian living books and poems that will inspire people to believe in Jesus for years to come. I simply live to wear the CROWN and help others wear the CROWN, too. The use of these pirate stories is a fun way to introduce people to faith, hope, and love. I pirated the heck out of these stories.

What Is BASK?

ask: To be in the sunshine, to enjoy the situation, to relax, to lie in glory. Synonyms: To delight in, derive pleasure, enjoy, savor, comfort, and rollick.

The author's take on BASK:

Bless: Bless the LORD with your soul (mind, will, and emotions).

1

Bless the LORD, O my soul; And all that is within me, *bless* His holy name!

2

Bless the LORD, O my soul, And forget not all His benefits:

3

Who forgives all your iniquities, Who heals all your diseases,

4

Who redeems your life from destruction, Who crowns you with lovingkindness and tender mercies (Psalm 103:1–4).

Ask: Ask Him for what you need. (A pirate meets his needs in his own way; the believer trusts God to meet his or her needs.)

24

Until now you have asked nothing in My name. Ask, and you will receive, that your joy may be full (John 16:24).

Stay: Stay Believing, Stay Abiding, Stay Steadfast.

57

But thanks *be* to God, who gives us the victory through our Lord Jesus Christ.

58

Therefore, my beloved brethren, be steadfast, immovable, always abounding in the work of the Lord, knowing that your labor is not in vain in the Lord (1 Corinthians 15:57–58).

5

"I am the vine, you *are* the branches. He who abides in Me, and I in him, bears much fruit; for without Me you can do nothing (John 15:5).

Know: That God is for you! Know the assurance of your salvation and the assurance of answered prayer:

11

And this is the testimony: that God has given us eternal life, and this life is in His Son.

12

He who has the Son has life; he who does not have the Son of God does not have life.

13

These things I have written to you who believe in the name of the Son of God, that you may know that you have eternal life, and that you may *continue to* believe in the name of the Son of God.

14

Now this is the confidence that we have in Him, that if we ask anything according to His will, He hears us.

15

And we know that He hears us, whatever we ask, we know that we have the petitions that we have asked of Him

(1 John 5:11–15).

This is what it means to "BASK." We bask in the Lord, and we delight in His glory and presence! We walk in the Light, as He is the Light! We live as children of the Light!

Bless, Ask, Stay, Know! Bask. This is the way to be truly Alive, Rich, and Free!

Pirate Speak

Insights that will help you break the pirate code!

Addled: *To be mad or insane, maybe just plain stupid*

Ahoy: *Hello*

Avast: *Hold fast, stop and pay attention*

Aye: *A pirate way of saying yes, but ye never really know if he means it*

Begad: *By God!*

Bilge: *The lowest part of the ship inside the hull along the keel; thus, nonsense or foolish talk— how low can you go?*

Bilge-sucking: *Uncomplimentary expression*

Blaggard: *An insult or a scoundrel*

Blouse: *A loose-fitting shirt*

Booty: *Loot*

Boucan Knife: *A quick-strike weapon used to hack and slash to overpower others, kept hidden under the blouse*

Buccaneer: *Caribbean pirates*

Bucko: *Used as "me bucko," "my friend"*

Bunghole: *Food was stored in wooden casks, and the stopper in the barrel was called the bung. Pirate food was bad, so being called a bunghole wasn't a compliment.*

C or Sí: *A Spanish pirate term for "yes!"*

Cap'n: *Short for Captain*

Cat-o'-nine-tails: *Or cat, for a whip made of nine leather straps used for flogging; it will smarten you up!*

Chase: *Ship being pursued*

Cockswain: *The Cap'n's attendant, one who would do the rowing*

Corsair: *A romantic term for pirate*

Crow's-Nest: *The platform near the top of the mast, a position for a lookout*

Cutlass: *A curved sword*

Cutter: *A single-masted sailing vessel that is rigged fore and aft with two or more head sails.*

Dance the Hempen Jig: *To hang from a noose made of hemp*

Davy Jones's locker: *The bottom of the sea*

Dead Men Tell No Tales: *A dead man cannot betray you with their secrets; therefore, a pirate would much rather turn them into shark bait, so that they could not bite them back by telling something incriminating.*

Doldrums: *Your ship is on the sea with no wind in your sails. A time of inactivity and stagnation, life* is dull, listless, and the crew is depressed. When sailing men are in the doldrums, you just never know what stupid things they will do.

Doubloon: A Spanish gold coin

Feed the Fish: When you are thrown overboard

Freebooter: A pirate, one who seeks to live free by plundering others, a buccaneer

Gangplank: A removable footway between the ship and the pier, also known as the gangway

Gangway: "Get out of my way."

Go on Account: To become a pirate

Godspeed: Good-bye and good luck

Grog: An alcoholic drink; pirates prefer rum

Hornswaggle: To cheat or defraud; to act like a pirate

I or Aye: "Yes"

Jolly Roger: The pirates' skull and crossbones flag, an invitation to surrender

Kiss the Gunner's Daughter: punishment; to be bent over a cannon and flogged

Lad, Lass, Lassie: Someone younger than you, e.g., a boy or youth, a girl or young woman (lass and lassie are females)

Land Ho: A sailor's cry to announce the sight of land and a way to say "watch out, rum, here I come."

Landlubber: "Lubber," an old English term for being big, slow, clumsy, not very skilled, as if they said, "I bet you were no better on land."

Letters of Marque: *Papers used by a national government, entitling a private seagoing vessel to raid enemy commerce*

Maroon: *To be abandoned and deserted; a convenient way for pirates to get rid of someone without actually killing him*

Matey: *A cheerful and friendly pirate address*

Me Hearties: *A way a Cap'n would address his crew*

Picaroon: *A Spanish term of derision meaning a rascal*

Piece of Eight: *A Spanish silver coin that could be cut into eight pieces*

Pillage: *To raid, rob, and sack*

Pirate: *A seagoing robber and murderer*

Port: *A seaport*

Privateer: *An armed private ship authorized by a country's government with Letters of Marque to attack foreign ships. Often their goal was to capture foreign ships rather than sink them. They were paid to raid, and then they would divide the loot with their sponsoring government, the investors, and the crew.*

R or Arrrr: *Glee*

Rum: *A traditional pirate alcoholic drink*

Sail Ho!: *"I see a ship."*

Scuppers: *Spaces on the deck edge which allow water to drain back into the sea*

Scurvy: *A disease caused by the lack of vitamin C; a bad sickness, and a derogatory term, "ye scurvy dogs"*

Sea Dog: *A very experienced sailor, one with lots of stories to tell, stories that always get bigger and better with time*

Shark Bait: *Your foes are about to feed the fish, or a worthless and lazy sailor, a "lubber."*

Shiver Me Timbers: *Shock or disbelief, perhaps from the shock of running the ship into a reef or from being hit with a cannon ball*

Shipshape: *A well-organized ship, under control, finished, or complete*

Sink Me: *Surprise*

Splicing the Main Brace: *After a strong storm or a fierce sea battle, when the main brace that held the main sail was broken, it would have to be repaired. It would have to be spliced together with another pole. This was dangerous work. Ropes would have to be held steady, and hemp rope would be used to wrap or splice the brace. The man in charge would reward this effort by giving his sailors an extra ration of rum. Today this phrase is a euphemism for "let's go get drunk."*

Swashbuckling: *Having the exciting manner or behavior of pirates, especially those depicted in films (obsolete, **swash** to make the noise of a sword striking a shield + **buckler** [shield])*

Walking the Plank: *A severe form of punishment where someone would be forced to walk a long and narrow piece of wood (a plank) off the boat and end up making a splash in the cold wet water. AKA "shark bait."*

Yo-ho-ho: *A pirate thing to say*

1.

BASK Your Way to Satisfaction

Wanting to find Peter to talk with him about his affections for his beautiful daughter, Esther, Tim looked everywhere around the house and the garden and finally heads to the beach. To his surprise, he sees Peter at the water's edge, making some peculiar hand gestures. He watches from a distance and observes Peter lifting his hands in what looks like praise. Then he lowers his arms and lifts out his hands as if he is begging for something; then he turns his hands to the ground and acts like he is pushing down, and he crosses his arms across his chest and nods his head affirmatively.

Tim has no idea what Peter is doing, so he finds a perch on a felled tree and just watches these unusual actions. Then again Peter lifts his arms, hands, and his head toward heaven and seems to be in a praise posture. He follows this move with hands cupped and reaching out as if he is asking for something. Tim then notices Peter turn his hands down as if he is driving down tent stakes into the ground. Then he crosses his arms, smiles toward heaven, and just stands there basking in the early morning sunrise, looking like a radiant angel.

Not wanting to interrupt what seems to be a sacred moment, yet feeling desperate to talk with Peter about his daughter, Tim slowly walks down the crags and makes his way to the beach, ironically walking in the same footprints that Peter has made. As he nears Peter, he whistles, as he doesn't want to startle him. He just wants to have an appointment with him. When they are eye-to-eye, Peter smiles and welcomes Tim and lets him know that he is happy to see him.

Tim asks, "What kind of ritual are you doing here?" Peter laughs and answers, "I am basking in the sunshine of God's love for me." Tim says shyly, "Really?"

Peter waits a moment and then says, "This is my way to 'walk in the light.' You know, light is who we really are. Jesus said that we are lights in this world, and I believe Him, so I just soak up the sunshine of His love with four simple steps." Tim asked, "What are those four steps?" Peter said, "I lift my head, my heart, and my hands toward heaven to bless the Lord. He is the source of all my blessings, so I bless Him with praises and thoughts about thanksgiving. Then I drop my arms and lift out my hands and ask God to meet my needs. I have found that I don't need to chase everything on my own when God wants to meet my needs, so I ask Him to. I think about a few concerns or needs I might have or others might have, and I specifically ask Him to meet those needs. I leave these requests at His throne of grace."

Tim said, "*Shiver me, timbers*, I had no idea we could talk with God like that." Peter said, "Tim, this is no religious exercise. This is just one friend talking with another." Tim asked, "You mean, you talk with God like He is your friend?" Peter said, "That is the truth. He calls me friend, and it is my highest honor to have God as my friend." Tim shook his head in amazement and then said, "You really do walk with God, huh!" Peter said, "Yes, I do. I call it basking in the Lord's presence. I bless the Lord. I ask Him to meet my needs, and then I affirm my commitment to Him by driving my hands down as if to say, 'I am going to stay believing in you. I choose to abide in You.'" Tim said, "I get it. Your prayer goes both ways. You show your commitment to God, and God ... hmm, hmm." Peter stepped in and said, "And God blesses me with His presence and affirms His commitment to me. The last thing I do is to tell Him that I know He is with me, for me, loves me, and has salvation taken care of for me. So, I cross my arms over my chest as if God is hugging me, and together we affirm that I know He is with me and for me. This makes all the difference in my life." Tim smiled and began to make the gestures. He lifted his arms toward heaven. He opened his hands as if to ask God for something, and then he plunged his hands toward the ground, and lastly he crossed his chest and nodded his head. He said, "That is all it takes, huh!"

Peter smiles at Tim and begins to sing as he gazes at the glistening ocean:

Thou burning sun with golden beam,
Thou silver moon with softer gleam:
O praise Him, O praise Him
Alleluia, alleluia, alleluia

Thou flowing water, pure and clear,
Make music for thy Lord to hear,
Alleluia, alleluia!

Let all things their Creator bless,
And worship Him in humbleness,
O praise Him, alleluia!

Tim was impressed and said, "That is simply beautiful." Peter said, "Thanks, I think we are to be like the moon; we are not the sun. The sun makes light. We are like the moon, as we only get to reflect the light of the sun. This is why I bask in the sunshine of God's love for me. I want to live reflecting His glory. You know the 'righteous are radiant.'"

Tim said, "I have never thought about it like that." Peter said, "From Francesco, I learned how God shows us His character in nature. His songs always speak of God displaying His glory in the natural world." Tim was slow in responding and stood silent for a moment and said, "Wonderful."

Peter paused and let the silence speak, and then he opined, "I think basking in the sunshine of God's love is a simple way to enjoy our relationship with God. It is really important to go to God with all of our needs, lest we expect others to meet our needs." Tim was stymied by that comment, and it showed in shyness. He waited and said, "I came to talk with you about Esther. I love her and want to be with her." Peter smiled and said, "I am so glad you have a good friendship." Tim said, "I just don't want to sin." Peter said, "I get it. It is better to marry than to burn." Tim said, "Thanks, how did you know?" Peter said, "I have had those feelings, too."

After some silence and awkward verbal stumbling, Tim looks for some smooth stones and begins to skip them off of the ocean. Peter also begins to skip some stones, and then he comments, "We can get these stones to skip two, three, four and some even five times, but then they all sink." Tim said, "They all take the dive." Peter asked, "What do you really want with my daughter?" Tim was pressed, and sweat drops formed on his forehead. Wiping his brow, he asked, "I want Esther to be my wife." Peter said, "Very good, young Tim. I will be pleased to give my beautiful daughter to you, but you must know that she cannot meet your needs, because only God can. Do you know this?"

Tim was set back in his thinking and said, "I haven't thought of it that way. I like her cooking. She is beautiful, and I love being with her. I don't want to be without her. I don't think I will ever find a person as fine as her. I know I want her." Peter said, "That is all well and good young Tim, but are you going to pressure her to meet your needs?" Tim said, "I hope not." Peter said, "Most men are like pirates and want women to meet their needs. Cook their food, help with their chores, have their children, and have sex when they want it. Are you going to be pirate in your dealings with my daughter, or are you going to be a real man?" Tim said, "I intend to be a real man. I don't want to be a taker like a pirate."

Peter had made his point, and Tim was now in a whirlwind of thought, so Peter, in a relaxed tone said, "Tim, I am not about perfect. I think you are a fine young man, but you have a lot to think about. Marriage will bring the worst out of you, but by God's design, it will also bring the best out of you. I would be honored to have you as a son. The only thing I ask of you is that you learn to bask your way to satisfaction."

Tim was wide-eyed and amazed. Had he just heard Peter give him his pledge to have his daughter? He thought so. In humility he said, "I will love her as Christ loved the church and gave Himself for the church. I know this means sacrifice. I will be counting that cost, and I am a man of my word." Peter said, "I can't ask for anything more. If Esther wants to be married to you, you will have my blessing. I just want to be able to lead you in the most excellent way."

Tim said, "Peter, you have been showing me the way. I want to learn from you. I admit I am young, and I don't really know everything that is going on in my heart." Peter said, "There is nothing more satisfying for a man than to have a love relationship with a godly woman. If you two will bask in God's presence, and each of you reach up to Him, you will be a triangle of His love with Him at the apex. As you draw close to God, you will be closer to each other. You do know that a strand of three cords is really one rope, which is not easily broken?" Tim nodded his head affirmatively, and then Peter concluded, "I am sure you will enjoy God together, grow together, and find Him to be your satisfaction. You have my blessing."

Looking out onto the water, Peter said, "Our relationships are a reason to trust in God. This is God's plan." Then looking out upon the ocean, Peter continued, "See the light jumping off the caps of the waves?" Tim responded, "Yes, I do. It is beautiful." Papa encouraged him, "It is about reflecting God's light. If you do this, you will have a wonderful relationship with Esther." Then Peter, while looking out on the sea, began to sing:

Rising, Dazzling, Reflecting
"Light of the World,'" You
Shine in us.

So I will
Glisten for Your glory!
Listen to Your story
And bask in Your love.

Because of Your Son
I am going from
Faith to faith
Hope to hope
Strength to strength
Glory to glory.

Rising, dazzling, reflecting
"Light of the World"
You shine on us.

Righteous and confident,
Alive and free,
The life of the godly
Shines bright eternally.

Because of Your Son
I am going from
Faith to faith,
Hope to hope,
Strength to strength,
Glory to glory.

Rising, dazzling, reflecting
"Light of the World," You
Shine in us.

So I will
Glisten for Your glory
Listen to Your Story
And bask in Your love.

This life overcomes
Victory is in me
I believe it
I live it.

Rising, dazzling, reflecting
"Light of the World," You
Shine in us.

It is who You are.
And, who I am in You.
Faith to faith,
Hope to hope,
Strength to strength
Glory to glory

Because of Your Son, I am
Colorful, transparent,
Cheerful and radiant
I come to light
This is Your life.

So I will glisten
In Your glory
Listen to Your story
And bask in Your love.

2.

God Is the Ocean of Delight

Up with the chickens, Chase and Tim make their way to Breeze's Café. The men enjoyed a plate of cackle fruit with vegetables and fresh-baked scones, smothered in butter and orange marmalade.

Whenever Tim and Chase get the time to talk, they always seem to reflect on their experiences on the *Adventurer*. Tim finds it ironic that the ship had to be decommissioned, and now some of its used timbers and old sails have been repurposed into the tent house they share as a home. Together they met Peter who was a Franciscan missionary on the island of Jamaica, who also was decommissioned as a missionary when he fell in love with Lily, a slave woman from the Ivory Coast. Then he developed a new kind of ministry befriending sailors and workers in Port Royal. He seems to understand pirate types, even though he is the anti-pirate—if there is such a thing.

Chase was aware of Tim's recent conversation with Peter and was happy about Tim and Esther's relationship, as she seems to be bringing the best out of young Tim. So as soon as Tim had his mouth full of eggs, Chase asked, "How did your conversation go with Peter? Did he give you permission to marry Esther?" Tim, looking over his cup of English breakfast tea, smiled and said, "I think so." Chase retorted, "What do you mean, 'you think so?' Did he or didn't he?" Tim lamented, "Well, what he cared about the most was something sort of new to me. He wanted me to make God my delight. He said if I delighted in God, everything would be right in my life, or at least that is what I thought he said. Do you know what he means?"

Chase was stuffing his mouth with a scone lathered in butter and marmalade, and with his mouth full of goodness, mumbled, "Let God be your all in all, your satisfier, the lover of your soul, and the delight of your life." Tim laughed uncontrollably, as Chase was so gleeful and lip smacking. Then he said, "I think Peter just wants to make sure God is real in my life and that I trust God to meet my needs." Chase said, "Yes, I am sure that is true, but there is more. I think he knows that for Esther to be truly happy, you can't be thinking that she is the source of your happiness. You have to come to the place where it is God who makes you happy, where He becomes your desire and your delight. You get your gusto from Him. You truly enjoy His company."

Tim remained quiet for a while, as he knew this was a serious conversation, even though Chase had marmalade dripping out of his mouth. Tim said, "You know, Chase, I have been thinking about how beautiful Esther is, how I desire her. I want her. So, honestly, you know that I love God, but I am crazy about Esther." Chase said, "You have hope matey, 'cause you are at least honest. Most men would rather *kiss the gunner's daughter* than be honest about the condition of their soul." Tim nodded his agreement, and then he said, "I didn't know Peter was a gunner!" Chase laughed, choked up some scone, and then said, "I don't think Peter was a gunner, or a son of a gunner. I do think he is a good and godly man. You could do worse, a lot worse." Tim said, "That is straight shooting."

Chase said, "You know the Bible says somewhere that 'God satisfies my mouth with good things.' This breakfast sure was good. I feel satisfied. Maybe there is a lesson here. What do we let fill our lives? We want God to fill our lives, His presence and His provisions." Tim said, "I get it, just as this food tasted so good, we are to taste and see that the Lord is good." Chase followed up, "That is it, brother!"

After a few moments of contemplation, Chase said, "You know it does say, 'Delight yourself in the Lord.' I think that means 'make God your delight.'" Tim said, "I think that is right. Wouldn't any other way be idolatry?" Chase said, "That is true. We need to think about this idea of delighting in God."

Tim said, "When I think about Jesus, I think about His names to try to understand Him better. His names tell me who He is." Chase said, "*Ahoy,* that is a good way to think about delighting in God. Let's dive deep into this idea." Tim agreed, "Let's think about His names and see if they help us to delight in Him." Chase said, "Great, what about Jesus being 'light'?" Tim said, "What a delight light is. I mean warmth, guidance, and the ability to see. It shows off the beauty of God's creation." Chase said, "Peter is always talking about basking in the sunshine of God's love." Tim said, "I know. He really believes God is light." Chase said, "And this truth is making all the difference in his life. I mean, you can see Jesus in Him." Tim said, "I know. He really reflects the glory of God."

Chase said, "So, light is an easy way to make God our delight. He makes light and has given us Jesus as 'the light of the World.'" Tim said, "If God didn't love us, we would be in darkness. Think about it: We wouldn't really have life at all, huh?" Chase said, "True shooting. I think light causes growth. I don't know anything that grows in darkness." Tim said, "Maybe some deep sea monster. Ever hear of the Kraken?"

Chase laughed and nodded his affirmation, and then he took another smothered scone and stuffed his mouth and said, "How about Jesus being the Bread of life?" Tim laughed and said, "I love the story of the manna from heaven. Jesus is the bread from heaven!" Chase was still chewing and trying to swallow his scone, and then with a mouthful said, "He really satisfies!" Tim said, "Yes, I love fresh baked bread. Esther makes the best bread." Chase said, "Enough about Esther." Tim said, "I am just saying the truth." Chase said, "Think about it: Bread really meets our needs. It has the grain, and the glorious smells, and it tastes so good." Tim said, "Taste and see that the Lord is good!" Chase said, "I think we are starting to see that God is the one who made life beautiful. He made tasty and good things for us to enjoy. He is even a lover of pleasure. He is truly delightful!" Tim said, "You don't sound like an old sea dog." Chase said, "I need to give Patch some credit for showing me these finer things. That one-eyed old man sure had a vision for the glory of God."

Together the men began to recall some of their favorite names they knew about Jesus. Tim had been able to read the Holy Scriptures and acquire some knowledge, but Chase could only pack away some of the names he had heard. Chase said, "Jesus is our Immanuel. God is with us!" Tim said, *"Aye,* a good name, indeed!" Chase continued with his list, "Master, Savior, King, Shepherd, and Teacher." The men took some time to meditate on what these names meant to them and to discuss how these identities could help them to experience God more fully. Then Tim added, "I have read that Jesus is the 'I AM,' the Deliverer, our Passover, and our Advocate." Chase had a number of questions about the meanings of these names and began pondering the meaning of each title. The men enjoyed diving into understanding the significance of these names.

Walking back to the harbor, Chase notices the vines growing up a tree and said, "Look here, and see the vine? Jesus is the vine, and we are branches." Tim said, "It is wonderful how we see Him in everything. He is the true Vine." The men once again took some time and enjoyed talking about Jesus being the vine, and we are branches. They both recalled how Peter regularly mentioned letting the sap flow by soaking up the sunshine. Together they realized that Peter's consistent teaching from nature, in reality, was magnifying the Lord.

They found a fallen tree not far from the water's edge and continued reflecting on the names of Jesus. Tim recalled that Jesus is the Priest, the Redeemer, Mighty God, Prince of Peace, the Anointed One." The men were in no hurry to get anywhere, so they just talked about what these names meant to them. While they were talking, Chase was reminded that Jesus is the resurrection and the life. The men talked about what happened to Jesus after He died on the cross, and that He was raised from the dead. They discussed how they were going to be resurrected in the future because of this truth. Their excitement began to build, as this time of fellowship had been so enlightening. Then Tim said, "I remember another name. Jesus is the Desire of All Nations." Chase said, "Yes, He is. It is just that most people don't know that He alone can satisfy their desires." Tim said, "I grew up in a Christian family. I knew a lot about Jesus, but it took that stinky ship and those *bilge-sucking* pirates to get me to look unto Jesus more deeply." Chase said, "It is true. Our trials can get us to get out of ourselves and look up to God. Or, if we fail to look unto God, we turn our thoughts inward, and we implode with depression." Tim said, "How did you get such deep thoughts?" Chase said, "Old Patch helped me learn to think. You do know that rejection causes anger, and anger turned inward is depression?" Tim just nodded his head.

After they were back on the dock, Tim said, "I laughed so hard this morning when I saw the marmalade from that sticky scone smeared all over your face. You were really enjoying it. I think that is how we are to be with God. We are to delight in Him by letting Him drip off of our faces, too." Chase chuckled, "Yes, I was savoring Wyndolyn's scones— so fresh, warm, and filling. 'C.C'. taste and see that the Lord is good." Tim said, "Maybe this is what Peter is getting at when he talks about delighting in God? You know: basking in the sunshine of God's love."

Chase agreed, "Most people would think we are *addled,* if they listened in to us blabber, but we can know and enjoy God this way. He made us for Himself. He made us for friendship with Himself, and our souls are satisfied when we let God be our all in all." Tim said, "How true, enjoying God is the true way to be happy. I don't always live this way. You know, I fleshed out a bunch on the *Adventurer.* The 'little pirate' shows up in me." Chase laughed and said, "We had a time, didn't we, but we believe that our souls are never truly satisfied with what this world has to offer. Wonderful friends, even a beautiful and godly wife is but a glimpse, but God Himself is the real satisfier." Then looking out onto the bay, Chase said, "Old Patch told me that 'these reflections off the water are glistening and warming rays, but

God is the sun. There are streams, creeks and channels, but God is the ocean of delight.'"

Tim said, "Amen! I heard my hometown pastor say 'magnify the Lord.' He explained that like with a spyglass, everything looks bigger. He said, 'When we magnify the Lord, He becomes bigger to us, and our problems get smaller.' I think that is the lesson for me today." Chase then asked, "How then do we magnify the Lord?" Tim said, I think talking about the wonderful names of Jesus has helped." Chase said, "Yes, and basking in the sunshine of His love, as Peter says, is a good way, too."

Chase leads Tim down the dock to see the salvage operation they have just about completed with the *Adventurer*. Chase showed Tim all the piles of lumber they have stripped off the *Adventurer* and the materials they have salvaged and are going to repurpose. Then he pointed out to the sea where the ship was sunk. He said, "She is buried there. She is a reef that can help secure this harbor." Tim said, "Good, maybe she will do something good. She only meant evil for me." Chase laughed, "We did have an adventure on the *Adventurer*, didn't we? There was no delight on her, but God is our ocean of delight."

Tim was taking it all in, pondering these wonderful and big thoughts about God that come from thinking about the names of Jesus and gazing out on to the ocean. He is quickened in his spirit and says, *"Sink me!* We need to remember that Jesus is the Water of Life."* Chase chimed in, "Yes, He is the living water, and because of Him, we thirst no more." Tim said, "Amen, brother! I will never forget those barrels of tainted drinking water in the bilge of the ship. No wonder we were so sick." Chase said, "Fresh living water is the gift of life to us."

The men stood basking in the sunshine of God's love, and with radiant faces, gazed out upon the big ocean. With gratitude in their hearts, they smiled toward heaven, realizing that God is the ocean of delight. Together the men began to ruminate over some wonderful thoughts about God and His glory. The ocean sights gave them inspiration and these thoughts followed.

Like diamonds
The brilliance
Rays that glisten
Luminance listens
Look and see

Light gives vision
Glorious sight
Splendid views
Enjoy the hues
Bask in God's love

God is light
No darkness at all
Bask in His love
Fellowship, delight
No bleak night

Live in the light
God is light
Splendid and bright
Dazzle in His sight
Bask in His love

Righteous and radiant
Bright is our sheen
Lean and gleam
Light to be seen
Bask in His love

Viva the light
The sap flows
The tree grows
Glossy fruit shows
Life so sweet

Like diamonds
The brilliance
Rays that glisten
'Tis the sunshine
Of God's love
Bask in His love

Bathe in His mercy
Relax in His grace
Jesus' blood cleans us
Forgiven and free
Believe and see
Grow like a tree
Bask in His love

His light shines
Life abundant
Love so strong
Like diamonds
The brilliance
Bask in His love

Like a cow chews its cud and then regurgitates and redigests its cud again, Tim and Chase were amazed at the beautiful thoughts they had been thinking. They enjoyed thinking glorious thoughts about God over and over again. Tim said, "Chase, you didn't speak even one pirate word." Chase laughed and said, "Well, blow me down."

3.

Wedding Preparations

Papa Peter was happy for his children, but wanted to offer up some instruction before these two lovebirds made their way to Kings River Falls and beneath the waterfall entered into the covenant of Christian marriage.

Knowing that Tim and Esther's relationship was cultivated in the garden, Papa hoped that he could meet with them under the shade of the magnolia tree and explain some of God's ideals to them regarding relationships and, specifically, Christian marriage.

As was their custom, Tim and Esther were in the garden early to avoid the heat of the day. Under wide-brimmed straw hats and their hands taking to their hoes, they were pulling up weeds as they worked their way down the rows of maize. Peter was encouraged to see how they were actually working and happy to see how they enjoyed talking with each other as they turned up the soil. Their joy was evident, and it gave them strength for their task. This setting of fruit trees, the garden patch, the turquoise ocean water as the backdrop, and framed by Jamaican blue skies gave this picture an "Eden's" feel.

As Peter entered the garden, he paused for a few moments just to observe and to give thanks. He basked in the moment, smiled toward heaven, and asked God to give him the wisdom he needed to impart the godly counsel that was in his heart. His head was also covered with a straw hat, and his limbs were protected by a long-sleeved white linen shirt. Papa sat until they finished working some rows, and then he approached the couple with his winsome smile and blessing. After hugs and kind words, Peter nodded toward the large magnolia tree that offered a huge canopy of leafy protection and asked, "May we take some time to talk?" Esther volunteered, "I will gather a pitcher of tea and some cookies." Both Peter and Tim were happy with this overture.

As Esther was strolling toward the house, Tim said to Peter, "I haven't asked her to marry me yet." Papa then pulled Lily's wedding ring out of his pants pocket and said, "Do you want to get after this or not?" Tim offered a hurried, "Thank you," and then sprinted to the house with the ring in hand and knocked on the door. When Esther opened the door, Tim was on his knees with a big smile and his hand was stretched toward Esther with the ring. Esther was delighted and full of joy. She asked, "What is this?" Tim said, "It is a wedding ring that God has provided. Will you marry me?"

Without hesitation Esther said, "Yes, yes, I will be your wife." With joy inexpressible, Tim and Esther enjoyed a long jubilant embrace complete with a long kiss. As they were hugging, they both remembered that Papa Peter wanted to meet with them under the magnolia tree. Esther asked Tim to carry some sugar cookies, and Esther carried the pitcher of tea to the magnolia tree where Peter was waiting patiently. Seeing his children with radiant smiles and skipping along, Peter just knew their lives were about to be transformed by Christian marriage.

After Esther set the pitcher down on the stump, she was happy to show Papa the ring. Papa asked, "Do you recognize this ring?" Esther then stared at it, smiled, and said, "I think so. Was it mama's?" Papa said, "Yes, and I am certain she would want you to have it." This remembrance caused the group to humbly pause and reflect on how precious life is. Papa said, "She would be very happy for you two today." Esther looked at Tim and then took his hand. Tim smiled big and asked, "Peter, did you want to talk with us about something?" Peter said, "Yes,

I do." They found places to sit under the shade of the big tree. After Esther poured the tea, they gave thanks and partook of the sugar cookies.

Peter, knowing that his children were young and unprepared for marriage, reckoned in his mind everyone is unprepared for marriage, and then he blurted, "I just want to take some time to prepare you for marriage. The Bible has so much to say about this subject, so maybe we can get started today." Tim nodded his head affirmatively, but he couldn't take his eyes off Esther, and Esther was just happy to cuddle up next to Tim.

Peter said, "You have been working this garden together, so I thought I would simply point out some lessons from gardening that pertain to relationships. After all, Jesus taught us so much about life and relationships from nature, and so did Francesco." Esther knew what Papa meant, and she indicated she was interested to learn. Tim was in a daze.

Papa said, "From gardening, you have learned to cultivate the soil. You need to keep tilling up the soil of your hearts if you are to have a healthy marriage. Healthy things always keep growing; so amend the soil with the nutrients of faith, hope, love, encouragement, and forgiveness." Tim said, "Yes, I agree; that is good." Papa said, "The Indians would place small fish in the holes with the seed when they planted to provide each plant with fertilizer." Esther asked, "Did they really do that?" Papa nodded and said, "They knew it gave the plant an assist." Tim just nodded his head and smiled. Then Peter said, "The good seed you are to plant in your relationship is the Word of God. It is imperishable and undefiled, and it will produce the fruit of righteousness in your lives and please God and bless you." Esther said, "Amen."

Papa asked, "What did you spend most of your time doing in the garden?" Tim laughed and said, "Looking at Esther and listening to her sing." Peter laughed and said, "I mean work-wise?" Esther said, "We pulled a lot of weeds." Papa asked, "In your relationship, what weeds will you need to remove from your lives?" Tim was dumbfounded and asked, "What do you mean?" Esther chimed in, "Things like critical attitudes, unbelief, and selfishness." Tim said, "Oh, I get it. How about laziness and worry?" Papa said, "Very good. You get the idea. We must plant the good seed, fertilize, and water." Tim said, "We didn't have to water." Papa said, "I know this lush Jamaican soil and our monsoons made it so that God did the watering for us." Esther said, "Isn't the water the current of grace you talk about?" Papa answered, "Yes, Esther, and in marriage, you will need to release much grace to each other. This constant favor, though unmerited, is only done by allowing the Holy Spirit to flow freely in you."

Papa could tell that he wasn't getting very far along with this illustration, as they had other things on their minds. He said, "To keep this garden fruitful, we have to keep the pests away, and I want you to think about what those pests might be. Tomorrow let's meet again right here and talk during this siesta time. I think you two want to go to the beach. Tim said, "Thanks, Papa." Then looking at Esther, he said, "Let's talk a walk to the beach."

Hand-in-hand and without any worldly concerns, their joy knew no bounds, as they made their way to the beach. Jumping in the blue waters, the couple was enjoying fresh freedoms because of the commitment they had made to each other. They both felt fully alive and thankful to God for good health and the blessings that were flowing into their lives. On their stroll home, Tim talked about how great it was to have Papa Peter's blessing. Esther, looking at her simple wedding band, spoke about how significant it was to have her mother's ring passed on to her. She said this would always remind her of the godly heritage her mother gave to her, even though she died while giving birth to her. Both Tim and Esther were touched as they reflected on this story of faith.

As they were walking back, Esther was reminded to think about the question regarding pests that Papa asked them to think about. She asked, "Tim, what pests do you think we will have to keep out of our garden if we are to flourish?" Tim said, "What? Where did that come from? What pests?" Esther said, "You know, Papa talked with us about tending to our relationship as we tended to the garden." Tim said, "Oh, yeah, *sink me*! I don't think I was paying attention." Esther asked, "Well then, what were you thinking about?" Tim grinned from ear to ear, and said, "I was thinking about how I am the most blessed man in the world to have you the most beautiful young woman in the world to be my wife. I was thinking about being with you." Esther sighed and came by his side. Their hands meshed and their stride slowed. They really didn't want to get home, as they so enjoyed being together. They didn't have words to describe their feelings, but they were feeling satisfied and fully blessed.

Walking along, Esther asked, "What do you think the pests will be that we need to keep out of our lives? We don't want anything to come between us." Tim said, "I don't know. I know my mom and dad struggled with money. They had concerns about food for all of us to eat, and that is why I had to go to work when I was little. But, here in Jamaica, we don't need to worry about food. We have a garden." Esther said, "This is true, but there are always testings, as there are always blessings."

Neither one could sleep because of their excitement about the future. Early they met in the garden and had a mind to work. When the sun shone bright, true to his word, Papa was there to meet with them under the shade of the magnolia tree. Once again Esther had prepared tea and fresh baked bread for their time. Papa asked them about their time at the beach and their conversations. The couple volunteered their thoughts about possible pests in their "garden." Papa talked about God's faithfulness and His plan for marriage. He used a triangle to illustrate how God is at the top and the man is on one side and the woman on the other. He explained like on the triangle when a man moves away from God, he gets further away from the woman, too. He also said that as they move closer to God, they would be close to each other. This was a picture they would value.

Papa said, "I have brought a passage of Scripture to share with you, and Tim would be familiar with it." He read from Ephesians 5:15–33:

15

See then that you walk circumspectly, not as fools
but as wise,

16

redeeming the time, because the days are evil.

17

Therefore do not be unwise, but understand what
the will of the Lord *is.*

18

And do not be drunk with wine, in which is
dissipation; but be filled with the Spirit,

19

speaking to one another in psalms and hymns and
spiritual songs, singing and making melody in your
heart to the Lord,

20

giving thanks always for all things to God the
Father in the name of our Lord Jesus Christ,

21

submitting to one another in the fear of God.

22

Wives, submit to your own husbands, as to the Lord.

23

For the husband is head of the wife, as also Christ is
head of the church; and He is the Savior of the body.

24

Therefore, just as the church is subject to Christ,
so *let* the wives *be* to their own husbands in
everything.

25

Husbands, love your wives, just as Christ also loved the church and gave Himself for her,

26

that He might sanctify and cleanse her with the washing of water by the word,

27

that He might present her to Himself a glorious church, not having spot or wrinkle or any such thing, but that she should be holy and without blemish.

28

So husbands ought to love their own wives as their own bodies; he who loves his wife loves himself.

29

For no one ever hated his own flesh, but nourishes and cherishes it, just as the Lord *does* the church.

30

For we are members of His body, of His flesh and of His bones.

31

"For this reason a man shall leave his father and mother and be joined to his wife, and the two shall become one flesh."

32

This is a great mystery, but I speak concerning Christ and the church.

33

Nevertheless let each one of you in particular so love his own wife as himself, and let the wife *see* that she respects *her* husband."

Tim smiled and asked, "Is that out of Ephesians?" Papa answered, "Very good, Tim, it is from Chapter 5. As you have heard, this is a rich Bible text. Let's start with the reminder that because the days are evil, and we all can let the 'little pirate' ruin us; we need to be wise. This is my prayer for you."

Tim said, "Thanks, Papa." Papa said, "One of the best things I learned about relationships came from my Franciscan brothers, as we would sing our way through life. The simple songs we sang helped me to keep Christ central in my life. It is amazing how these Scripture-filled songs can give uplift to our thoughts and words. So the apostle reminds us to have melody in our hearts. I think our words must be kind and sweet. So make it your aim to say nice things to each other and let your tone be tuned into God's grace. If you do this, you will feel loved, and isn't this why you want to be married, anyway?"

Esther said, "This is really important. I have heard the men down at the dock shouting obscenities at the women; it makes me cringe." Tim said, "It is cruel speech. You should have heard them on the ship." Esther said, "That ship life was messed up."

Papa continued, "The lesson here now moves to submission: Submission is contrary to the pirate way. Pirates always act independently and do their own thing. Christian marriage requires obedience to God and to each other. It is about humility and regarding the other person more as more important than self. Husbands are to submit to God and to their wife, and the woman is to submit to God and to her husband. This is about yielding our own desires to God and to the other. It is about showing love and respect all the time. Tim, you have a big responsibility here. God is asking you to nurture Esther in such a way that you will present her to God in all her glory."

Tim was quiet, and then he spoke, "I haven't been thinking about marriage that way." Papa said, "It's not just about hugs and kisses. Christian marriage is about growing in Christ." Esther laughed and said, "I am glad we are thinking about this now." Papa said, "Our joy level is always in accordance with our commitment level. This is why we are reminded that Christ's love for the church required His sacrificial death. And now His joy is great, as He sees us loving Him and each other freely. This is why

He died for us, and I believe He is happy to see you grow together." Tim said, "I am glad it all adds up to joy. But, I wasn't aware of all the responsibility and sacrifice required of the man."

Papa said, "Jesus loved His bride. His bride is the church; the church is us, and He gave his life for us. This Bible text concludes with a reminder to the woman to show respect to her husband. It is all about love and respect. Love is the action a person takes to express and reflect the character of God. Respect is the attitude, and the actions we make are to show high regard, esteem, and value to another. Esther, this is very important to the man. Your husband needs to be respected by you." Esther said, "I understand this." Papa said, "I know you do, and I am happy that Tim is not a pirate. It is impossible to respect a selfish pirate." Tim said, "I promise to not be like a pirate in our marriage." Papa said, "Very good. Esther, you can respect Tim because He is made in God's image. He is a child of God by faith in Jesus, and He wears the crown."

Tim was humbled and quieted by these truthful comments; he shyly bowed his head and opened his hands to heaven because he was basking in the Lord's presence. Papa said, "We have covered some ground today. We will continue tomorrow right here under this magnolia tree. I am certain that you know love and respect is the way to go. It is the way to experience satisfaction. I know that God has made every provision available to you for you to have a successful marriage."

Esther sensing that Tim was overwhelmed by the responsibilities of marriage said, "Tim we have the power to have a healthy and long lasting relationship." Tim lifted his head and said, "I know we do, but God will have to help me." Esther said, "We have the power, we have His life." Tim smiled and his eyes began to twinkle as he observed Esther's confidence. Esther took Tim's hand and opened her beautiful voice and like an angel she sang. :

"By faith
We have the power
The power of an endless life

We have been told
About streets of gold
We are the bold
Never to be sold
This never gets old

When absent from
Our bodies.
We will be present
With the Lord

With Jesus,
We have the power.
The power of an endless life.

His love is endless
His promises are endless
His life is endless

Not by human might
Or fleshly power
By the Spirit we delight in,
The power of an endless life

By faith
We have the power
The power of an endless life

We have been told
About streets of gold
We are the bold
Never to be sold
This never gets old

The worries of this world fade
Temporary things
Lose their claim

The power of an endless life
We break free
From the bounds of earth
And empty pursuits

Child-like faith
Sets us free to forever bask
In the sunshine of God's love

We will never be disgraced
Ultimately we win it all
We are the people of God
His Word abides in us

Because we have the power
The power of an endless life
We have an inheritance
Heaven is our home

We have been told
About streets of gold
We are the bold
Never to be sold
This never gets old"

Tim applauded the beautiful song and said, "I don't know what I liked more, the truth in the song, or your faith being expressed?" Esther swooned, and the couple embraced. Papa Peter said; "You two are a great pair."

4.

White Waterfall Wedding

*T*im, while lying in bed, couldn't get over Papa Peter's promising words. Papa said, "I believe every provision has been made for you to have a successful marriage." This hope-filled thought had Tim thinking and going over it again and again in his mind. Having lived the way that he had and having been on the *Adventurer* with a band of flesh-driven *scurvy* pirates had taken the innocence away from Tim, and not to mention his garden surprise. Tim was fearful with regard to what he was bringing into his upcoming marriage with Esther. Fear has a way of creeping in to destroy and disrupt our joy. Tim was vacillating between hope and fear. He wanted to choose joy, but fear was trying to harpoon him and take him under like a gasping and blubbering whale.

As he meditated on the phrase, "every provision," he thought about how Jesus had forgiven all his sins. How he had the Holy Spirit's presence and power in his life. How the Bible gave him guidance, complete with promises and instruction. How Papa and the church community were providing them with good models, encouragement, and support. "Shoot fire!" Esther loves God, seeks after God, and loves Him, too. What could go wrong? We have every provision!" And, on top of it all, he had real love in his life, and love never fails. He thought, "By God's grace, we can do this." All the cultural differences, racial differences, sexual differences, past failures, and background concerns began to fade, as Tim focused his thinking on the unity of the Spirit and the bonds of peace Papa talked so much about.

Esther loved being loved by Tim and was longing to make a home with Tim. She envisioned raising children and family time around the family table. She thought about ways they could do ministry together in the Port Royal community better together. She smiled as she thought about long walks on the beach with Tim and cool evenings holding hands and cuddling by a fire. Esther had been reading the Song of Songs in the Bible and was raptured by the romance and beautiful sensuality that leaped from the pages like the gazelle she read about. Esther was looking forward to her wedding day, because she had dreams that she knew God was going to fulfill in her life. She just knew that Tim was a great catch: He was handsome, considerate, caring, and completely Christian. Her concern was all about herself: Could she satisfy his desires?

Even though Tim was excited about his wedding day, he was getting "cold feet." He knew that his heart was filled primarily with sexual thoughts. He had lusted and coveted Esther's beautiful body, and still he reviewed the image of her bending over in the garden while she was picking beans and left her breasts uncovered and in full sight. Tim just knew that he wanted to dive in to that luscious garden Esther had for him. His feelings of inadequacy, and the reality of his carnality, made him feel way too "pirate-like' to be the husband he knew God wanted him to be and Esther needed. He wanted to get married so badly, but his motives were so mixed and tainted. He loved Esther, but he thought, "She is longing for relationship, family, and the time to talk about sweet things, and I want to dive in sexually." The truth about his desires caused him to go to God and be honest about his sexual passion. He knew he loved her as a person, but questioned if he could love her if she wasn't so darned beautiful and sexually attractive?

Tim's doubts began to surface, but he had to suppress them because the church community was celebrating their engagement. They got together to affirm their upcoming marriage with gifts and prayers of blessing. Some of the ladies brought handmade utensils and bowls made out of wood as wedding gifts. Chase brought a tallit and presented it to the couple. He explained that this Jewish prayer shawl was a covering the man would use by taking his wife and children under it as a canopy and praying over them. Chase explained how the man provided his wife and family with cover and protected them with his faith and his life. He explained how the man's family loved this expression and mentioned that it was good for the man, too, because it reminded the man that it was God who was the covering for his family. Chase also mentioned that the man was to impart identity and a sense of destiny to his wife and children and talked about how this tallit would help with that purpose. This tallit was a beautifully embroidered cloth with images of the menorah candle and the Star of David.

To conclude the service, Chase and Papa took the tallit and laid it over Tim and Esther and prayed for them. This was a really important time for Tim, because he knew that he needed God to cover him. Chase's comments, though they were thoughtful, were also weighing heavily on young Timothy. He knew how immature he really was and how impure he was in his heart. However, he was choosing to believe that God's grace was greater than his fears; yet, he was making the choice to believe that his adequacy to be married to Esther was Jesus in him, and not his past failures, and even his present fears. He was choosing to believe that God had made every provision for him to have a beautiful relationship with Esther.

The next day, this winsome church family gathered in the garden to bring in some of the crops and do some extra weeding because the couple would be gone for awhile. They made commitments to pray for the couple and to watch and work in the garden while they were away. Tim and Esther had planned for a honeymoon in the Blue Bay on the other side of the island of Jamaica. To get there would require a river ride down the Rio Grande and lots of hiking and camping. They were going to travel light. They had made a simple tent out of old sails from the *Adventurer,* and Esther had put together a bedroll to sleep in. Tim had a fishing line and was sure he could learn to catch their food. After all, he reckoned God could feed them from the trees, as there was fruit everywhere. If they needed meat, he thought he could find and skewer some turtles, as turtle was a staple in these parts.

Tim, Esther, Papa Peter, and Chase, along with Frieda, began the hike up to the Kings River Falls in the cool morning air. This trek was a walk through paradise, as the pink, blue, yellow, and red flowers were graciously basking in the sunshine and serving as a bouquet to host this ceremony. As they got nearer to the falls, the rumble of the river only served to excite Tim and Esther about their impending nuptials. Papa once again talked about the river and the current of God's grace, as he was always enraptured with Jesus' word picture of the river flowing in us. Frieda was a happy witness to this event. Everyone sensed that she knew what was going on, and she chirped away to express her pleasure.

When they arrived at the river, they sat down on fallen logs to gaze upon the beauty of this heaven-made sanctuary. The steady flow of water over the cliff made a beautiful cascading sound, and the mist caused the moss on the rocks to glisten in the sun. After eating sugar cookies that Esther had made in the shape of a crown, they enjoyed drinking the water and rested for a few minutes. Then Tim and Esther began to stake up their tent and Chase began to gather some wood for a fire. He noticed that others before him had left a pile of wood under the canopy of a big tree. He was thankful and replenished the stack.

Tim put on a white linen shirt for this occasion; as he buttoned it up, he thought about the significance of white. He paused and reflected about waiting till marriage to engage sexually, and how faithful Jesus had been to keep him chaste, pure, and a virgin, even though he didn't always feel this way. This was the truth. Esther stayed in the tent, making Tim and Papa, Chase, and Frieda wait. Papa said, "Tim are you ready for a lifetime of waiting? Marriage will teach you to wait." Tim laughed and said, "Esther is worth waiting for!" Papa said, "Remember that years from now." Tim nodded his understanding and said, "I get your point." Then Tim began to tear up. He pulled the sacred sheets of Holy Scripture out of his pocket and handed them to Papa for the ceremony. He said, "My family couldn't be here, but these pages are from our family Bible. They serve as a witness from Mom and Dad and my family." Papa was touched by this overture and said, "Tim, this Word has seen you through and will uphold you in the days ahead."

Through his tears, Tim looked up to see Esther opening up the tent flap and walking out dressed in a simple long white dress. She was radiant and elegant, and Tim began to choke up as he thought about the blessing she was to him. She was holding yellow flowers in her hand, and her hair was flowing back with a band of light blue flowers. She was stunningly elegant, and with courage and grace, she walked toward Papa. Tim, Chase, and Frieda were on the side. Tim was blurry-eyed. Esther's beauty had him weakened, and when she saw his eyes, she knew his heart was awakened. Then she noticed the sheets of Scripture and lit up with a big smile. She knew what they meant to Tim and how God's Holy Word was central to their lives.

Papa opened the wrinkled sheets of Scripture and read from Ephesians 5:

25

Husbands, love your wives, just as Christ also loved the church and gave Himself for her,

26

that He might sanctify and cleanse her with the washing of the water by the word,

27

that He might present her to Himself a glorious church.

Papa asked, "Tim, do you take Esther to be your wife, and do you promise to be faithful to her?" Tim answered, "I will."

Papa then asked Esther, "Esther, will you take Tim to be your husband, and will you be faithful to him as long as you live?" Esther answered, "I will." And then Papa said, "Tim, you may kiss your bride." The couple swooned in an embrace, and then Tim planted a generous kiss on Esther's lips. The couple stayed embraced for a good while. Chase cheered, and Frieda squawked, but Papa said in jest, "Kissing don't last, but cooking do." Esther, rolling her eyes, said, "Come on, Papa." Then Peter said, "I am happy for you. God is pleased, and you two will be a blessing to many. This is a highlight in my life." Tim and Esther could tell that Papa was beginning to choke up with emotion. Then Papa said, "It has been good to talk with you about Christian marriage. In thinking about your relationship and your future, I wrote a song for you." And then he sang:

EVERY PROVISION
Every, every, every
Every provision has been made
We can live victoriously
We can be joyous
You will see
Jesus died for you and me

The blood of Jesus
Has paid for all our wrongs
Justified by faith
The truth of it all
He paid the big debt
We are free indeed

Every, every, every
Every provision has been made
Not enough has been said
He wants to freely give
Only believe and see
Every provision has been made

Every, every, every
Sin is taken out of the way
Laws couldn't change our hearts
The Spirit of life in Christ
Sets us free to live
Without dread
Forgiveness is in the provision

Satan uses lies
And guilt to malign our identity
No longer an effect on me
Because I am saved and free
Satan shames and accuses
To no avail
We prevail

Every, every, every
Every provision has been made
Grace and mercy are my friends
Failure has no sting
Now I can attempt great things
His acceptance makes me sing

Every, every, every
Every provision has been made
Catch the vision
Glory is our reason
I'll walk with God
His Word not forsake

Every, every, every
Every provision has been made
Victorious Savior
Heaven is assured
Trials shrink in prayer
Every provision has been made

Bask in the sunshine of His love
Every provision has been made
Keep your eyes stayed on Him
He will lead the way
Just stay, just say,
Every provision has been made

Every, every, every
Every provision has been made
Broken souls made new
False starts are through
O, sink me
There is
New wind in sails
We will prevail
Because
Every provision has been made

The couple cheered the song and the singer, and they talked about the blessing in it. Papa said to Chase, "It is time for us to go." The group held hands, and Chase offered a prayer. He said, "May God bless you and keep you. He will watch over you and give you grace and peace in the Holy Spirit." Frieda squawked with glee, and they began to walk back down the hill to Port Royal. Papa couldn't help but look back at the couple, and Tim and Esther were holding hands and waving back with tears in their eyes, too. Papa cried all the way home, but Chase and Frieda were there to humor him along.

Tim and Esther looked at each other with satisfaction in their eyes. The both realized that they had just received a tremendous blessing from Papa and Chase, but were humbled by the realization that God was cheering them on from heaven. This heavenly setting was affirming God's grace to them. Together, hand-in-hand, they walked to the water's edge and began to swim out to the falls. They enjoyed letting the water fall on their heads, just as His grace was cascading upon them from heaven. There they played with the water and each other for a good while. Holding each other in their arms and whispering sweet nothings and blessings, observing the beauty all around them, giving thanks and also observing the gift of a loving life mate. This experience could only be described as ecstasy. They both affirmed that this level of pleasure and satisfaction was because of God's love and design. Holding each other, they prayed and thanked the God of heaven for His blessing to start to their new life together.

Earnestly they made their way back to the tent. Esther went in to change, and Tim started a fire. Esther brought bread and jerk chicken in her basket, and the two enjoyed sharing dinner and sitting by the fire and basking in the light of it. They kissed each other profusely, and in little time, they were inside the tent and entering into the act of marriage. In only the light of the moon, they were naked and unashamed and enjoying the pleasure God reserves for a man and wife.

5.

The Tallit and the Tent

Tim and Esther were happy to wake up in each other's arms. Having consummated their wedding vows with the act of marriage in their makeshift tent, they were happy as could be, but very surprised.

Esther was surprised to discover how excited Tim was to enjoy her sexually. She had heard people talk about sex and brought with her to the marriage bed some of those bad thoughts, but was happy to have experienced something beautiful with her lover that could only be described as God- ordained.

Even though viewing Esther's voluptuous body aroused Tim, he wasn't surprised by this experience, as he had been fighting off this urge for months. But what surprised him the most was how inviting she was, and how she, too, enjoyed being sexually intimate with him. He knew that they looked at this act differently. Tim enjoyed the thrill of it and the sense of being a real man. And, he knew Esther wasn't driven like this, but liked the time together and feeling valued, understood, and loved.

Together they were surprised to realize that though they were different, they enjoyed a precious unity of the spirit. Their bodies are different—the man's and the woman's so different from each other's—her color is different from Tim's, and their cultural differences were worlds apart; yet, together they are now one flesh. Truly they have a great friendship, and with Christ at the center of their relationship, they have a love that is unusual to this world.

Because of this world, each one had been corrupted with regard to their attitude toward sexual intimacy. Tim, having been around pirates, had to deal with the thoughts of conquest and had learned to become a selfless giver and a caring man. Esther had to resist the mindset of the women in the sex trade and not use sex as a tool, but to hold dearly this unifying gift from God that sex is God's gift in marriage. Yet, thanks to God, their church community, and Papa Peter, this couple was able to enter into their marriage tent with wisdom and appreciate the innocence that was theirs. They knew that they had emerged this morning still innocent and pure in God's eyes. The act of marriage is a pure experience for those who are knit together in God and hold to their vows.

These virgins are still virgins in many ways, as they, by God's grace, have not been destroyed by this dirty world. They are happy that they saved themselves for their wedding night. This morning they are sitting by the fire enjoying their English tea. Esther says, "Tim, you are a real fire starter: You started one last night in our tent and this morning." Tim laughed and answered, "My passion was satisfied by you. You give me fire." Esther was happy to know that her husband was happy with her; inwardly, she worried that she wasn't enough for him. She smiled and said, "We are blessed, and I am so happy that God has given me you." Tim said, "I am the one who is blessed. You got the bad part of this deal."

Esther said, "I think we will see that God has given us every provision for us to have a good relationship." Tim said, "I agree! Let's pray together." Then taking Esther's hand, he offered up a tender prayer of thanks to God, and Esther followed Tim's prayer with, "Thank you, God, for Tim, and his role in my life. We commit this marriage to you." Tim said, "Yes, Lord, we thank you, and we trust you to lead in our marriage."

After their tea, Esther said, "I brought something special for you." Tim said, "What did you bring?" Esther got up and went to her satchel in the tent and brought out some papers she had written on. When she brought them to Tim, Tim was very impressed with her beautiful script, but surprised by their content. Esther said, "I have written out several passages from The Song of Solomon for our honeymoon." Tim asked, "Why did you do that?" Esther said, "Let me read them to you, and you will know." Tim said, "Well, *ahoy!*"

Esther began to read from the first chapter of Song of Solomon:

2

Let him kiss me with the kisses of his mouth—For your love *is* better than wine.

3

Because of the fragrance of your good ointments, Your name *is* ointment poured forth; Therefore the virgins love you.

4

Draw me away!

Tim asked, "Is that really from the Bible?" Esther replied, "Yes, this is from King Solomon. It is the Song of Solomon." Tim resounded, "*Shiver me timbers,* I had no idea." Esther said, "In this next passage, you will see me."

5

"I *am* dark, but lovely, O daughters of Jerusalem,
Like the tents of Kedar, Like the curtains of
Solomon.

6

Do not look upon me, because I *am* dark, Because
the sun has tanned me. My mother's sons were angry with me; They made me the keeper of the vine-
yards, *But* my own vineyard I have not kept."

After a moment of silence, Tim asked, "How
are you in that passage?" Esther said, "See, I am
dark." Tim said, "And lovely." Esther kissed Tim on
his head, and then she took the pages and read from
the second chapter:

4

He brought me to the banqueting house, And his
banner over me *was* love.

5

Sustain me with cakes of raisins, Refresh me with
apples, For I *am* lovesick."

Tim said, "I am hungry." Esther said, "Yes,
your activity in the tent made you hungry." Tim
smiled, and said, "Hungry, yes, but satisfied." Esther said, "So I will make you some raisin cakes and
refresh you with apples." Tim asked, "Does this verse

mean that our lives are to be a celebration?" Esther responded, "Yes, I believe so. He loves us and has made every provision for us." The couple then gathered some fruit from the trees, and from her supplies, Esther put together a meal for the couple to enjoy. After eating, the couple decided to stay beneath Kings River Falls and enjoy the setting, each other, and God's Word. The hibiscus flowers were in bloom, and the waterfall was glistening as it reflected the sun. The couple chose to bask in this setting and just enjoy being young and alive. Tim went in the water and enjoyed swimming around and under the falls. The running water reminded him of God's constant flow of grace into his life. From behind the falls, he looked at Esther sitting by the water's edge, reading and writing. He could only thank God for this wonderful person God had given him.

Esther brought with her bag with some thread and needles to embroider designs into the tallit. So along with a blue Star of David and a silver menorah candle, this tallit was about to receive some red hibiscus flowers from Esther's hand and creative mind. Tim said, "You are full of surprises. What else do you have in that bag?" Esther laughed, "I will delight in keeping you on your toes." Tim said, "I know you will. Do you have any other surprises for me today? Those Scriptures opened my eyes. Is God a pleasure lover?" Esther answered, "He must be. After all, He made chocolate." Tim said, "No, you don't have chocolate, do you?" And then Esther opened her bag and unwrapped some fine Belgian chocolate the trade winds brought to the port. She said, "I purchased this for a special occasion. And this is special." Tim said, "Yes, it is. I love chocolate. But I love you more." Esther smiled and then received a kiss on the lips from Tim.

After they wrestled a bit, Esther said, "I do have another surprise, and then she took out of her bag what looked like a diary and said, "I wrote a song for you this afternoon." Tim said, "I can only take so much." Then Esther replied with a smile, "Tell me what you think." And then she sang:

Beloved
Dressed in white
Beautiful sight
Come away with me
I do, I will
My beloved

Beloved
Come away with me
My beloved
Gone through so much
Come and touch

Beloved
Come away with me
Thought I'd never love
Let me be your dove
We are loved

Beloved
Come away with me
I want to feel alive
No need to strive
Be surprised

Beloved
Naked and unashamed
Accepted and loved
Touch me like a man
I am your beloved

Chorus:
His grace, His plan
You are my man

Beloved
I care for you
Won't judge you
Come away with me
My beloved

Beloved
Lost in your love
Deeply, deeply lost,
Found safe by your side
Really loved

Beloved
Come away with me
A strand of three
Knit by His hand
We will stand

Beloved
Come away with me
Build a home
We are not alone
Let love show

Beloved
My darling, hold me tight
This is right
Come away with me
My Beloved

Chorus:
All I want
Is to see your face
Hear your voice
Enjoy your touch
Have your trust
Taste your love

Tim applauded and then took her by the hand and held her tight. The two enjoyed dancing to the rhythms of the waterfalls and being married. Tim went about gathering wood to build a fire and thought of Chase, because Chase had left a good pile of wood for them. Tim thought that it would be good to collect some wood for the pile for who would be here next.

6.

Coconuts, Chocolates, and Limes

Being young and in love is the most envious situation one can have. Tim and Esther know that they are blessed to have each other and especially blessed to have had the support of family and their faith community. But, today they are newly married and naïve about how to relate to each other. They are now one-flesh and on a learning adventure about God's plan for love and marriage. They are thrilled to be married and truly love each other and can't quite believe how good God is to give them a wonderful partner.

Tim is enthralled with Esther; their wedding night was beautiful in every way. By God's grace they had been saved for each other and were grateful for the virgin innocence they enjoyed. Esther was pleased to see that Tim was truly excited about her and was delighted in his response to her. Tim is amazed to discover that Esther desires him sexually, and Esther is happy to know that Tim treasures her as a person, and not just for the sexual pleasure they have experienced.

To be alone with each other and free to show love as a man and wife was the yearning in their hearts. Their Christian community had embraced them, but now they are on their honeymoon and on their own. The reality of cleaving is exciting to them, but now the reality of leaving has placed a thud in their souls. There is no one to go to for support. All of a sudden, they realize that all they have today is each other and God. While sitting by the fire, they talk about this situation and hold each other tighter and exchange kisses.

While holding each other, Tim prays over Esther and commits their marriage and their new day to God. Esther says, "Tim, that makes me feel good. We need to keep going to God and sharing our lives with Him. I was feeling alone, even though you are here, and God is here. Not having Papa and our church family makes me feel weak." Tim said, "I know. I am so happy to be married to you, and I know God wants us to get to know each other, but I have never had an adventure like this." Esther said, "We really need to talk with each other. I need to know what you are thinking about and what makes you happy."

Tim said, "We need to discuss our plans. I think not knowing what we are doing today is *blaggarding* me." Esther said, "I agree. Let's talk about our plans."

The couple sat by the fire and had a good long talk about their honeymoon to Port Antonio and the Blue Bay. They both realized that they had been so focused on their wedding day that they had failed to develop a day-by-day plan. Tim liked being spontaneous, while Esther needed to know what they were going to do that day. While they were holding each other, Tim experienced an epiphany and was beginning to understand that Esther wasn't as time-oriented as he was. She was content to take her time, bathe, and brush her hair. Tim wanted to get after it, and he wanted to get down the trail to the Blue Bay.

Patience wasn't a virtue Tim had much of, but that was about to change if he wanted to experience the full cup of pleasure God has for him. So after they had a good talk, they swam out to the falls and played in the water. The falls reminded them of God's continuous flow of grace into their lives. They enjoyed ducking under the falls and looking out and seeing the beautiful prism of colors formed in the skies around the falls. This spectrum of color in the foliage along with the hummingbirds and little critters climbing on the rocks around the falls made for an Eden setting. The couple delighted in knowing that Almighty God had given them this beautiful day to inaugurate their marriage.

One of the most important provisions Tim brought with him was an ax; he knew this was a useful tool for this adventure. So while Esther took time to ready herself for dinner, Tim took to the ax and climbed a coconut tree and knocked down some coconuts. With a couple of coconuts under his arm and his ax in his belt, he headed back to Esther to surprise her with coconuts. He lopped off the tops of the coconuts, and together they drank the sweet water from the coconut. Tim then took the ax and chopped the hard outer shell and carved out the meat of the coconut. Esther retrieved the Belgian chocolate, and they enjoyed coconut and chocolate for dinner. They both realized God had provided them a dinner treat reserved for royalty.

Even though Tim wanted to make some progress toward his goal of Port Antonio, he could read Esther's body language and determined that she wanted to stay the night. Tim just relaxed and allowed his soul to go at her pace and not his. He reckoned that, after all, she was his wife for the rest of his life, and it wasn't in his best interest to push her. So after sitting and admiring the falls and enjoying a delightful day at the pool, the couple decided to wander and look for more fruit in the area. They discovered that the trees were filled with produce;

mangoes, nuts, and limes were found. Tim plucked some limes and with the ax chopped them in two and squeezed the juice out into their canteen and filled it with fresh water from the pool.

As Tim was squeezing the juice out of the limes, he noticed that he just naturally threw the used-up carcasses of the limes away. They really enjoyed the lime drink they had made, but the picture of the used up lime skins made an indelible impression on Tim's mind. As he sat down to think and to pray, he realized that Esther was like the lime; if he squeezed her too much, he would throw her away, too. This horrible thought troubled him, and he sat and thought and took his thoughts to God in prayer.

His thought was about his sexual appetite. He had just had sex for the first time with Esther and, by being honest with himself, he just knew that his appetite for sex had him "howling at the moon." He was fearful that he, too, could become pirate-like—like most of the crew on the *Adventurer*—but what could he do to save his marriage, Esther, and his sanity?

When Tim got troubled, he had the tendency to withdraw and get quiet. But this was his honeymoon, and Esther wouldn't have it. She was in a playful mood and flickered her eyebrows and said, "Tim, my love, would you build us a fire, and we can rest here and then retire for the night. Then you can build another fire in the tent." Tim said, *"Shiver me timbers,* I will get on it." In no time, Tim had built a fire, and together they were cuddling up and enjoying the warmth of the fire and the fellowship of love.

It wasn't dark yet, so Esther brought out the pages of Scripture she had handwritten from the Song of Songs. As she opened up the folded pages, she said, "I am sure this will be new to you. It was to me. It has shown me a new understanding of God's love." Tim said, "I was amazed with what we read last night."

Esther pointed to the Bible text and read from the second chapter of Song of Solomon:

6

His left hand *is* under my head, And his right hand embraces me.

7

I charge you, O daughters of Jerusalem, By the gazelles or by the does of the field, Do not stir up nor awaken love, Until it pleases.

8

The voice of my beloved! Behold, he comes Leaping upon the mountains, Skipping upon the hills.

Tim was shaking his head in disbelief, and said, "Are you sure that is in the Bible?" Esther exclaimed, "Yes, this is the Song from King Solomon." Tim said, "That doesn't sound like he is hunting for deer; it sounds like the act of marriage. I'd never done it before last night, but I knew what to do." Esther laughed and said, "Yes, you did, and you know what to do. Do you see where the lover placed his hands? That is just what you did." Tim, shaking his head, said, "Yes, I am a quick learner."

Esther said, "Yes, you are, but what amazes me is God. God made the act of marriage to be enjoyed, and Solomon captures the joy of intimacy here." Tim said, "I am dumbfounded by this. I had learned that sex was dirty. The men on the ship were profane in describing it, and even my parents and my church talked about it being a wrong and shameful thing. It is confusing to me."

Esther paused and then explained, "I think people mean well. After all, sex is reserved for those in the covenant bonds of holy marriage." Tim said, "I know that is true, but I am the same man I was yesterday." Esther challenged his remark, "You think so? I think everything changed for us when we took those vows." Tim said, "What do you mean? I feel awkward about this. All I know is that I love you and like your body. I cherish your body; I think King Solomon was talking about a woman's body. Come on, 'gazelles'!" Esther laughed, "It is descriptive, isn't it?" Tim said, "Yes, I love the thought of God loving pleasure. Is this right? If it is, this changes everything for me."

Esther said, "I think this is big! God is a pleasure-loving God. After all, he made pleasure. Maybe this is because He truly is a loving father and wants us to enjoy Him and all that He has made." Tim got real quiet, and then looking at the falls, he began to explain, "Water, so enjoyable, made by God. He made chocolate and coconuts, and they are so good together. Lime and water, so good together. Tim and Esther, so good together." Esther cheered these comments and then said, "If God didn't love us, do you think He would have made chocolate?" Tim countered, "Chocolate is sure proof that God loves us." Esther said, "I believe God loves us and everything God made is good and to be enjoyed." Tim said, "Whoa, Nelly, that is rich!"

Esther said, "I know that is an exciting thought, but I think it is true. I just think we have to get Port Royal out of our heads." Tim said, "How good it is to be away from that wicked city. It has corrupted our lives. I know that I have thoughts of God being a demanding schoolmaster more than I thought of Him as a pleasure-loving God." Esther said, 'Exactly, but our born-again human spirits are not corrupted; we are holy people and capable of enjoying the beautiful, tasty, and delightful things God has made." Tim said, "Somewhere in the Bible it says, "Taste and see that the Lord is good." Esther said, "On our honeymoon, let's get Port Royal out of our lives. And believe that God is a pleasure-creating and loving God!" Tim held her tight and kissed her on the lips and said, "I really do love you, and your good mind is helping me see how good God is."

Esther blushed and said, "I have another Scripture. If we have enough light, we can read it. Then turning the page toward the fire, Esther read from the second chapter:

10

My beloved spoke, and said to me: "Rise up, my love, my fair one, And come away.

11

For lo, the winter is past, The rain is over *and* gone.

12

The flowers appear on the earth; The time of singing has come, And the voice of the turtledove Is heard in our land.

13

The fig tree puts forth her green figs, And the vines *with* the tender grapes, Give a *good* smell. Rise up, my love, my fair one, And come away!

Tim couldn't stand all this incredible goodness anymore; he took hold of Esther and said, "Come away with me, my beloved." And he carried her into the tent. Esther giggled and frolicked and together they thought about God being a lover of pleasure. They put their minds in a much better place than Port Royal.

7.
Shanghaied, Again

The goodness of God has captivated Tim and Esther. This honeymoon in the tropical paradise of Jamaica is beautiful in every way, but the glory of it is the pleasure they are experiencing. Certainly they are taking delight in the grandeur of this wondrous natural setting. The elegant waterfalls, the colorful flowers, and the entertaining birds and critters have opened their eyes to the creativity of God. The sensual delights they are enjoying are also gifts from God, who said that it wasn't good for a man to be alone. So He outdid Himself and created the woman. And just as Adam was pleased with Eve, Tim is very happy with Esther, even if she takes her sweet time to brush her hair.

Finally after a breakfast of English tea and hard scones, the couple is ready to begin their trek to Port Antonio and the beautiful Blue Bay. As they were hiking, they sipped on the limewater and had some chocolate for energy. They had to make their way through some heavy foliage, and Tim had his ax ready to do some chopping, but nothing had to be cut down. As was custom, they took a siesta during the heat of the morning and enjoyed resting in the shade. They found a lime grove and basked in the wafting refreshing fragrance on the breeze. Life couldn't be better.

Esther convinced Tim to make this their resting site and to call it a day. It wasn't that Esther was tired; she just liked the setting with the trees and the river nearby. Tim took a fishing line and went out to snag some salmon and was successful. Once again, Tim was able to find some firewood stored under a tree and had enough to start a fire. Esther gathered some native vegetables for the skillet and fruits for a salad. She pared these luscious items down with a knife, and in little time their dinner was roasting on the fire. The smell of the salmon in coconut oil on the fire and the vegetables evoked the feeling of royalty. This couple felt like the richest people in the world and were grateful that God had provided a beautiful dinner for them.

After a scrumptious meal, they went down by the river and just sat, watched, and listened. Then Tim said, "I feel like the richest person in the world.

We have had chocolate, limewater, and cooked salmon. The only thing better would be some sex for dessert."

Esther didn't smile or laugh. She looked disgusted and said, "Is that all you think about?" Tim should have left it alone, but said, "No, I do think of other things every now and then." Then Esther's countenance fell, and she mumbled, "What did I get myself into?"

A coolness came over the couple like the water they used to douse the fire. They stayed the night in the same tent, but they didn't touch, and they didn't speak to each other. Esther had no idea why her "beloved" had cooled to her; just the day before, they were on fire with passion and sizzling in their dialogue. Just as Adam and Eve were kicked out of Eden for their sinning, Tim and Esther had now self-inflicted themselves with needless isolation. Why couldn't they say, "I am sorry," or, "Please forgive me"?

The next morning, Tim grabbed his ax and his sharpening stone and sat by the river and continuously ran the stone over the ax's edge and thought about his life. As he sharpened his ax, his mind was taken back to the day he received a hammer blow to the back of his head and was *shanghaied* and forced to work as a conscripted slave on the *Adventurer*.

This memory has him going over and over it again and again in his mind, because he feels some of the same groggy and awful recollections from that dreadful experience. But the contrasts between these two days are palpable.

The rejection he experienced at the hands of pirate-types hurt his head and made his body ache. But, getting smacked with shame from the woman he loves hurts far deeper. When he woke up on the *Adventurer*, he was isolated on a stinky ship with strangers and far from his family and church community. Tim sees the parallels and reckons that he has been *shanghaied* again. But, who hit him? Was it Esther harpooning him with a shameful accusation? Certainly she didn't mean to take him down, or did she? Tim was perplexed and flummoxed. He just sat and sharpened his ax and thought about why he hurt so badly and why he wanted to stonewall and keep his distance from Esther.

Esther stayed in her tent and brushed her hair and looked into a little mirror she brought on this honeymoon, so she could look beautiful for her husband. Now as she looks into her mirror, she shakes her head negatively as she thinks about bad men. She is thinking that all men are bad. They are all pirate-like, and all they think about is sex. They reduce women to sex objects and don't value the relationship; they just covet the thrill of sex. She looks to heaven and says to God, "Father, what am I supposed to do? You want me to be cherished and not treated like the women in the whorehouses. I am not a whore!" She remains quiet before God and listens for His still but faint voice.

Tim has moved from the stump, where he sat sharpening his ax. Now he is down by the river, gathering stones to skip. He is looking for smooth stones, as he knows if he throws them just right, they can skip on the water four, five, and maybe six times. As he bounces these stones and knocks them around in his left hand, he has a thought of King David, who also picked up five smooth stones in his daring assault on the giant Goliath. He thinks about how this uncircumcised Philistine giant was profaning the name of God and taunting the young shepherd boy who had a clear advantage, because God was with David. Tim laughs and begins to skip these stones across the water. They really zip, and Tim's countenance is lifted up as he confesses, "God, why should I stonewall and withdraw? David didn't when he faced Goliath. Please help me lean in to this giant in my mind." After wearing himself out with rock throwing, he sits down and thinks about how he got *shanghaied* again. These thoughts come to him, and while standing at the water's edge and in the canyon, he humbly sings:

Shanghaied, Again

Darn it
Shanghaied, again
Knocked out and drug down
To the bilge below

Keelhauled
Belittled and conscripted
Mistreated and defeated
Laying low

Scraping barnacles
Off the hull
How low can I go?
Feeling numb in the skull

I have hope again
Sunshine in my soul
You make me whole
Fresh wind blows

Swab the deck
Drink the gruel
This is cruel
Wish I were back in school

Addled and gnarled
A bad word
A cannon's loose
Kiss the gunner's daughter

Darn it
Shanghaied, again
Who is to blame?
For this cloud of shame
I am in a shroud

What can be done?
I need to see the sun
Doldrums no fun
I have been shunned

Isolated, marooned
Shanghaied, again
I need to be saved again
To rise above

When hope seems lost
Can I believe again?
I can BASK in the sun!
Believe, Ask, Stay, Know

Hallelujah
Saved again and again
I bask in the sun
The sunshine of love
God is here

I am redeemed again
Basking in the sun
The sunshine of love
I believe
I ask
I stay
I know

I have hope again
Sunshine in my soul
You make me whole
Fresh wind blows

Tim takes hold of what has happened in his soul, and reckons that it is not the gale: It is the set of the sail that gets the ship in the current. He humbly admits that, in this case, he allowed himself to be *shanghaied* again by letting those unfortunate words take hold of the cargo in his heart. He acknowledges to God that he has let these petty feelings take him low into the bilge of despair and block him from having the fellowship he really loves with the love of his life, Esther.

Meanwhile, Esther is in the tent and is seeking God, too. She is miffed as to why her man left her, why he emotionally walked the plank away from her, and became cold toward her. She meditates on passages from the Song of Songs and her eyes of her heart are opened and she sees an image as to what she is to do. She reads from Chapter 3:

1

By night on my bed I sought the one I love;
I sought him but I did not find him.

2

I will rise now, *"I said,*
"And go about the city;
In the streets and in the squares
I will seek the one I love."
I sought him, but did not find him.

3

The watchmen who go about the city found me;
I said, "Have you seen the one I love?"

4

Scarcely had I passed by them,
When I found the one I love.
I held him and I would not let him go.

Esther still didn't understand that she had "shame-wacked" her lover. He took her words as a rejection, and he emotionally packed up and moved next to the river. She also didn't know that God was working in his heart to help Tim understand how he had to take responsibility for his own thoughts and buck up and be a man and begin to move back toward Esther again.

Walking out toward the river, seeking her lover, she hears him singing in the canyon. Her heart is thrilled, and when Tim sees her moving toward him, he bows out his chest, lifts up his arms, and begins to run toward her. They are so happy to meet each other, and by faith, the cold chasm is being bridged again by the cross Jesus died on.

The couple doesn't fully understand how shame tried to harm their relationship. But they are learning to accept each other and to be careful with their words.

From the second chapter of Song of Solomon Esther reads:

14

"O my dove, in the clefts of the rock, In the secret *places* of the cliff, Let me see your face, Let me hear your voice; For your voice *is* sweet, And your face *is* lovely."

16

My beloved *is* mine, and I *am* his. He feeds *his flock* among the lilies.

From the Song of Solomon, the eighth chapter:

7

Many waters cannot quench love, Nor can the floods drown it. If a man would give for love All the wealth of his house, It would be utterly despised.

8.

Boa and Butterflies

Esther found Tim down by the river skipping rocks. He had withdrawn from her emotionally and was not the spiritual leader she had hoped he would be. However, their love was great, and they did not subject each other to performance-based conditional love. The love that says, "I will only love you if you measure up to my standards and meet my demands." No, Esther reached out to Tim with God's unconditional love and hugged him and let him know that she was happy to see him and needed him to be with her.

Tim apologized for stonewalling and being distant and said, "I know I shrunk back from you, and I know that didn't please God, or help you. I am sorry. I was wrong." Esther was quick to offer up, "I forgive you, and I will try to understand. I know the 'rain 'a fall, but the duty tough.'" Tim asked, "What are you saying?" Esther said, "Here in Jamaica, we say, 'Sometimes the rain falls, but the ground doesn't receive the moisture. It stays hard.'" Tim said, "I get it. We have received so much from God, but we are not always thankful or understanding." Esther said, "*Ahoy, matey,* you understand that we need to let God's love and mercy sink into our souls." Tim said, "That is for sure. I have been skipping rocks, and with each hop of the rock, I am trying to understand why I did what I did, and why I felt what I felt." Esther said, "I will go back to the tent and get ready for our hike today." Tim said, "I will be there in a bit to pack things up."

While standing at the edge of the river and winging flat-sided stones, Tim begins to hum and sing:

I Am a Man
I am a man of God
A son of the living God
A royal heir of the King
I belong to Him

I renew my mind
I take my stand
I will lend a hand
This is who I am
I am a man

Why should I be swayed?
Why should I delay?
His Word is sure
My mind is stayed

I wear the CROWN
I am freed from sin
Blood bought and born again
I am a man of God

I say "to hell" with unbelief
I won't dwell on defeat
I will get out of my shell
To victory I set sail

I believe in prayer
I keep hope alive
I am all about life
I am a man of God

I am freed from sin
Seated in heaven
My deeds are from love
I am faithful and true

Mercy covers my mistakes
Grace gives me a retake
Depression I can shake
My claim is staked

I am a man of God
The price has been paid
My mind is stayed
I won't be played

I am a man of God
A son of the living God
A royal son of the King
I belong to Him

I am a champion
Not naïve to the negative
Enthusiasm is real in me
I have been raised with Him

I renew my mind
Take my stand
I will lend a hand
This is who I am
I am a man

By allowing the words in the song to embolden him, Tim takes to heart what he has allowed to happen to him. He begins to understand that Esther's comment about his sexual appetite made him feel ashamed, and instead of facing the music, he withdrew, got silent, and began to stonewall. He realized that he caused the distance in his relationship with

Esther and that he needed to take responsibility for his actions. He needed to tell his soul the truth and not allow flippant words to *shanghai* him, because he is responsible for his actions and to his wife. He now reckoned that he is a man of God and that he will live out of this truth—and not by the feelings that want to sink him and his marriage.

With renewed energy, resolve, and joy, Tim meets up with Esther and packs up the tent. He throws it over his shoulders and realizes that just as he is man enough to carry this pack, he is man enough because Christ is in him to shoulder his responsibilities as a husband. Once again the honeymooners are back on the trail and following the path next to the river and making their way to Port Antonio and the Blue Bay. Their conversation is sweet, and they are thrilled to have this day to walk, talk, and enjoy God and His beautiful creation in the tropical paradise of Jamaica.

After an hour or so of walking, they relax in a lime grove and luxuriate over the glorious scent. Joy has embraced them again, and they are having fun with each other. Then they see some deer down in a gully. But to their amazement, they observe a boa constrictor slither off a branch, wrap itself around a small deer, choke it to death, and then drag it further down into the gully, where it begins to feast on its prey. Tim and Esther couldn't believe the brutality they had just witnessed in nature. The snake amazed Tim, and Esther was frightened by the episode. The juices of adrenaline were now pumping in their veins, and they hightailed it out of the area.

When their legs slowed down and their lungs begged for air, they began to walk together at a reasonable pace. While still gasping for air, Esther said, "That scared the innards out of me." Tim laughed and said, "The boa choked the innards out of that deer." Esther said, "That didn't help me." Tim said, "I am sorry, but you have to admit that was gruesome, huh!" Esther responded, "I can't get that memory out of my mind. Seeing that poor little deer get strangled by that ugly snake is a terrible thought." Tim said, "I am sorry, beloved. Let's set up our tent and call it a day. We will rest and eat and be on our way tomorrow." Esther said, "That sounds good, but let's stay away from trees, I just can't be under a tree right now."

Tim went and caught a fish, gathered some firewood, and together they enjoyed a wonderful dinner under the stars. Tim was amazed at how helpful Esther is and told her so. He said, "Esther, I am so blessed to have you. You are so helpful. You know how to cook and sew. We are a good team." Esther smiled and said, "I think we are, but we need to learn how to talk and share our feelings." Tim said, "I know that is true. I know I clammed up back there." Esther said, "Yes, you did. I can't get that snake out of my mind. I see that deer being strangled, and I think about myself. I feel as if I got strangled, too." Tim said, "What?" Esther said, "I feel like I got strangled, too. I got strangled by your silence." Tim, wanting to hang his head in failure, but choosing to engage, said, "How is that?" Esther said, "As you went away from me and stayed away, I thought you lost your care for me. As you were silent, I felt unloved and began to choke up. I thought you might leave me, and it was killing me inside."

After some moments of quiet, Tim said, "I am sorry; I was just thinking about myself. I will think about you first." Esther had the tallit and needle and thread in her hands and just took time to stitch another flower into the fabric. Tim was quiet and took the sheets of Scripture out of his pocket and meditated upon a passage from Philippians, Chapter 1:

3

I thank my God upon every remembrance of you,

4

always in every prayer of mine making request for
you all with joy,

5

for your fellowship in the gospel from the first day
until now,

6

being confident of this very thing, that He who has
begun a good work in you will complete *it* until the
day of Jesus Christ;

7

just as it is right for me to think this of you all, because I have you in my heart, inasmuch as both in
my chains and in the defense and confirmation of
the gospel, you all are partakers with me of grace.

8

For God is my witness, how greatly I long for you all
with the affection of Jesus Christ.

After he let God's Word sink into his mind,
he went to Esther and shared this passage with her.
Together they drew strength from this Bible text as
they discussed it. Tim could tell that Esther loved
to hear from God, and she acted as if every time
God's Word was opened to her, she believed God
was speaking to her. Tim noticed her heart opening
to God and to him, just as a flower opens to the
sunshine. Together they were basking in God. Tim
said, "I thank God for you." Esther replied, "Tim, I
thank God for you, too. I am so happy that you are a
Word-filled man." Tim said, "I will always keep you in
my prayers." Esther smiled and said, "With joy, I will
keep thanking God for you. We, too, are confident

that God who has begun a good work in us will keep on working in us." Tim's eyes were opened, and he said, "I have read that passage many times, but I hadn't seen that promise before." Esther said, "This gives us confidence and assurance."

Esther said, "Seeing that boa constrictor attack that deer today made me think of a song about spiritual warfare that Papa taught me." She quietly sang it with her native Jamaican vibe, using her hands to pat the pot as if it were a drum.

Crushed It
Stay obedient to the Lord
Committed to do what is right
Stay innocent of all wrongs

Put on the full armor
Be strong in His might
Sing glorious victory songs

Let the God of peace
Crush Satan
Under your feet
Stake your claim and be
Alive, rich, and free

He crushes the enemy
With His Word,
By the blood and with
The authority of His name
We have no fear of shame

Our enemy is an
Accuser, liar, thief, deceiver
A monger of fear
The enemy of every believer

This serpent is a tempter and usurper
A snake in the grass
That seeks to make us gasp
Rebuke the devil
Live boldly
Out of a true identity
Raise your scepter high
Assert your authority
Stomp its head

Let the God of peace
Crush Satan
Under your feet
Stake your clam and be
Alive, rich, and free

Don't be oppressed
Sulking, pouting, and depressed
Swat that joy sucker back to hell
Don't dwell on the swell

Forsake the stress
Raise your sail and
Flow in the current of
God's grace

Jesus is the name that
Gets this enemy to run
His love casts out fear
Jesus is the one
Who paid the price!
Defeated that foe at the cross
Remember the blood that was shed
That cleanses and sets us free

Live free forever
Because He has
Crushed it
Live alive, rich, and free
This is our destiny

Tim applauded Esther's beautiful singing and commented, "Who would have thought that the enemy was going to mess with us out here?" Esther said, "This is why we need to constantly wear the armor of God." With that thought, the couple called it a night and slept peacefully as they thought about God being "the God of peace." God gave them a restful night's sleep, and in the morning, they enjoyed breakfast by the fire. They both were grateful for how God was at work in their lives and sat by the fire side by side when a bunch of butterflies landed on a log next to them. There were orange, yellow, blue, and even zebra-striped butterflies to admire. Esther explained, "Jamaica is famous for our giant swallowtail butterflies." Tim said, "I noticed them in the garden and am amazed at how easily they fly and fill the sky with their color and beauty."

Just as Esther was about to talk, the butterflies took flight and dazzled like light catchers, opening their wings and basking in the sunlight as they fluttered away. When Tim looked back at her Esther waxed on eloquently, saying, "I think these butterflies teach us how important it is to wait on God." Tim, shaking his head in disbelief, said, "What do you mean, 'wait on God?'" Esther said, "Come with me." And Tim followed her to the grove of lime trees, and Esther pointed at some worm-like creatures crawling on the bark of the tree. Esther said, "These worms are going to become beautiful butterflies." Tim said, "Have you been drinking rum?" Esther laughed and said, "No, but look: See how these worms spin and knit out a shell that becomes a co-coon? See these baglike things hanging on to the branch?" Tim looked and grabbed one and started to open it up. Esther said, "No, wait! It is in a process of transformation. It goes from worm, to cocoon, and in time, a beautiful butterfly will emerge." Tim said, "I want to see what is going on inside that sack." Esther said, "Look here: Here is one emerging, and in quiet awe they that sat there watching the crea-ture in the sack struggle to break free. And as they watched, the miracle happened: a beautiful butterfly emerged. It spread its wings and began to bask in the sunshine as it flapped its wings and flew away, just as God planned.

The couple went back to their fire, finished drinking their English tea, and talked about the transformation process they just witnessed. Tim was amazed and was excited to compare himself, their marriage, and life itself to the process a worm goes through to become a butterfly. Esther, always her daddy's daughter, tends to spiritualize. She said, "The worm was always a butterfly. It just needed time and struggle to develop." Tim's eyes sparkled with insight, and he said, "I get it! He who began a good work in the worm, is beginning a good work in us, and He is faithful to complete it." Esther chimed, "Bravo, Tim!" Tim smiled and lifted his shoulders in an "ah, shucks" kind of way.

9.

Riding in Freedom

arriage is designed to bring the best out of the man and the woman. Marriage will also expose the worst in the man and the woman. This is by God's design, to cause us to trust Him and to grow in Him. God is showing Tim and Esther His grace, and today they are enjoying a joy-filled walk along the Rio Grande on their way to Berrydale.

To make their way through some of the lush foliage, Tim is happy to chop away at some of the branches; this act makes him feel manly. He especially loves it when Esther asks him to help her carry her pack. For this journey, Tim has their tent on his back packed in a sack and his few belongings stuffed inside it. His ax is in his belt, along with his knife. And Esther has her pack and a bag with her belongings. Though they are traveling light, the load gets heavy because of their cooking supplies. So, Esther has Tim take one side of her pack, and they carry it together. They both don straw hats as they try to keep the hot Jamaican sun off their necks.

Tim has let the shame of yesterday evaporate like the fog off the river when the sun comes out to play. Today they are basking in the sun—and most importantly—in the light of God's love. The terrain is rough, but when the river comes into clear view, Tim's heart leaps with excitement because he observes people riding on the water. As curious as can be, he encourages Esther to make their way to the water's edge to see this happy sight. He wants to know how in the world these simple people are riding on the water.

This is a delightful sight. Tim observes people standing on bamboo shafts on top of the water and riding with ease and freedom. They hurry their way to Berrydale, appropriately named because it is a dale rich in local produce. Esther is thrilled to see the fruit stands, but all Tim wants to see is the rafts. And up next to the first fruit stand, he sees a raft, and he studies it like a scientist looks at an insect.

This is a very simple design for a raft: about two dozen bamboo shafts knit together with hemp rope. The raft is given stability by the rope that runs through the center of a smaller bamboo shaft that serves to buttress the shafts together. Then the raft can be stood on in the water, and with a long pole, the rafter can push off the river bottom and sail away, floating in freedom. The vendors use these rafts to bring their produce to Berrydale.

Tim is happy to discover that this river flows all the way to Port Antonio. In his mind, he catches a vision of building a raft and floating his bride the rest of the way. The Blue Bay is not far from Port Antonio. Tim looks around and sees bamboo shafts in the distance, and as he is walking to look at them, he sees hemp growing everywhere. He is immediately chopping these shafts down and pulling at the roots and gathering these hemp weeds. With just a little time and effort, Tim has all the supplies he needs to build the raft.

Esther has been enjoying herself at the fruit stands, talking with the people, when suddenly she realizes that Tim is not by her side. She earnestly looks for Tim, and he is not around. Then she looks down the way and spots him in the weeds. She goes to him and asks, "What are you doing in the weeds?" Tim says, "I am going to build you a raft, and we will ride the water to Port Antonio." Esther asked, "How are 'we' going to build a raft?" Tim said, "Look and see. It is a simple idea. We will take these bamboo shafts and knit them together with hemp rope." Tim then began stripping the wiry strands of hemp apart and showed her how they could be woven together as strong threads to make a rope.

Esther smiled and said, "I like this idea, and I can braid these strands like I braid women's hair." Tim said, "Bravo, Esther, that is all we need to do."

In no time at all, Tim and Esther were ambitiously working. Tim was aggressively slicing and shredding the hemp plants and handing over to Esther long strands for her to braid. Tim, with his ax, made a nail out of wood and drove it into a tree to create a hook for the braid to be held, so Esther could anchor one end and braid the strands efficiently. They were really proud of their efforts, and the afternoon flew by quickly. They had all the materials they needed to build what Tim was calling the *Adventurer*, a tribute to the ship he came to the island on. In his mind, this was redemption of sorts, as he really wanted to forget the motley crew and the stinky ship that tried to ruin him.

Dusk began to set in, and Tim and Esther decided to gather their materials, set up their tent, and prepare for dinner and camp here in Berrydale. While trying to tie knots, Tim noticed a familiar face in the distance, a face he would never forget. He said, "Esther, look, see. That is Nick 'Neck-beard.' He was on the *Adventurer* with me. I hope he doesn't see me." Tim lowered his head into his work. Esther replied,

"That is the ugliest beard I have ever seen. What is he called?" Tim said, "He is Nick 'Neck-beard'." Esther replied, "Why do pirates always make up names to go along with someone's physical characteristics?" Tim said, "I never thought much about it, but just as a pirate's words are few, they just don't think much about the real person, you know. They just look at the outside."

Esther said, "I think you are right. I have heard about 'Patch-eye,' Captain 'Hook-hand,' "Peg-Leg,' and even 'Red-Legs Greaves.'" Tim said, "A scary bunch, huh!" Esther said, "I wonder what they would have called you had they had a chance to name you?" Tim said, "They would have called me 'The Wave.'" Esther said, "The Wave?" Tim, while stroking a wave of his long blond hair said, "Yes, 'Tim the Wave.'" Esther just laughed and shook her head and said, "You are more like, 'Tim the Pale,' 'cause you are a paleface." Tim just shook his head, and then he looked up, and, standing in front of him was Nick "Neck-beard." Nick said, "Are you the conscript from the *Adventurer* named Tim?" Tim said, "Yes, Nick. Good to see you again."

Nick and Tim shook hands, and then Tim introduced Nick to Esther, saying, "Nick this is my wife, Esther." Nick said, "It is nice to meet you." Esther offered a gracious, "Nice to meet you, too." Then Nick asked, "What brings you here?" Tim said, "We are making our way to the Blue Bay for our honey-moon." Esther chimed in and asked, "Nick, would you like to join us for dinner?" Nick asked, "What are you going to have?" Esther said, "Whatever fish you and Tim can catch." Nick said, "I know where we can spear some bass."

Nick showed Tim how to make a spear out of bamboo shafts, and then they began sneaking up on some bass in the water. This was a fun sport, and Tim really enjoyed learning from Nick. While out on the water, Tim and Nick took some time to swap stories from the *Adventurer*. They really didn't know each other from the ship, but enjoyed hearing about their trip from the other's perspective. Nick also en-joyed hearing how Tim met Esther and was curi-ous to know what Tim meant by his phrase, "God brought us together."

Back at the campsite, Nick helped Tim prop up the tent and gather wood for the fire. They cleaned the fish, and Esther had the bass frying in coconut oil on the fire. Nick asked about the bamboo poles and the hemp rope that they had gathered, and he began to show Tim how to weave the shafts together and how to tie the knots, so they would have a sturdy ship. As the two worked together, in a couple of hic-cups, they had made some real progress on fashion-ing a seaworthy raft. Esther called the men to come to dinner, and the men with dispatch dropped the rope and the bamboo and joined Esther for dinner.

The dinner was scrumptious, and Tim and Nick took the skillet to the river to clean it. It was now dark out. As they were making their way back to the campfire, Nick asked Tim, "How can I get what you got?" Tim, not knowing what Nick was really asking, said, "A beautiful wife?" Nick laughed and said, "No, you really do believe that God is in your life, don't you?" Tim said, "Yes, I do." When they arrived at the fire, Esther, having overheard their conversation, asked to retire to the tent and to go to bed. Tim kissed her good-night and went back to sit on a log next to the fire and to talk with Nick. In reality, Esther went into the tent to pray; she just knew God was up to something.

Tim asked, "Nick, do you want to know God personally?" Nick responded affirmatively, "Is that really possible? Would God want me? I have been a disgusting pirate." Tim answered, "Jesus came for sinners, and He died to save sinners." Nick said, "Hell, I am one." Tim laughed and said, "The good news is that you don't have to go to hell." Nick said, "I think I have already been there. The ship life was hell." Tim said, "I know. I remember the rough life it was. I remember the stench and the cruelty." Nick said, "I've had the scurvy, and besides, I went along to get along." Tim said, "Ahoy, Nick. That is the first step

to being 'born again,' admitting that you need Him."
Nick, shaking his head, asked, "What do you mean,
'born again'?" Tim answered, "Shoot-fire *matey*, do
you want to know God personally?" Nick said, "Hell,
aye." Tim, in earnest said, "Jesus said, 'You must
be born again to enter the kingdom of heaven'." Nick
asked, "What does that mean?" Tim said, "Just as
you were born physically from your mother and
father, you must be born spiritually." Nick asked,
"How is that?" When you believe in Jesus, you are
born from above. The Holy Spirit causes you to be
born spiritually; by the Spirit Jesus will come to live
in you, forgive you, and help you with your life." Nick
said, "Sounds too good to be true. Can He forgive
me?"

Tim waited a moment and said, "God loves
you just as you are. All He wants you to do is believe in who Jesus is, what He has done for you on
the cross, and that He rose from the dead. If you
choose to believe this way, you will be born again,
and you will be a child of God destined for heaven."
Nick said, "How can this be so simple?" Tim smiled
and said, "God made it that way because he loves pirates and wants to save pirates." Nick said, "I believe
that Jesus died for my sins. I have heard about the
resurrection from the dead." Tim said, "Ask Jesus
to forgive you. He already has. He just wants you to

own it, be real, and then ask Him to come into your life and be your Savior."

Tim stayed quiet. Esther was in the tent praying, and then Nick looked to heaven and said, "Jesus save me. This is Nick, and I have been a lousy sinner and a sea dog." Tim shook his hand and said, "Brother, just believe that God is now saving you, and that you are a child of God." Nick said, "Whew, why was that so hard?" Tim said, "Because even pirates are a proud sort and don't want to admit that they need God." Nick said, "But I feel so free," Tim said, "Isn't that interesting? The reason men become pirates is to be alive, rich, and free. But, you have never been better off than you are right now." Tim offered up a prayer to God, and Nick was grateful to talk with God personally.

Tim said good-night to Nick and went into the tent to sleep with Esther, and Nick slept out under the stars, like he had a thousand times before, but this time he swore he could see them twinkle. With tears in his eyes, he began to thank God for this good news that he was able to believe. Esther rolled over and whispered in Tim's ear, "God used you tonight. I am proud of you!" They slept peacefully.

The next morning they enjoyed a good breakfast of local fruit and more fish. They all drank English tea and had a wonderful conversation about faith around the fire. Nick was happy to tell Esther about the decision he had made the last night, and Esther was full of joy for him. The men helped with the cleanup and then went to work snugging up the knots on the *Adventurer*.

After their siesta, they took the *Adventurer* up the river, and with Nick holding the raft, Tim got on her, balanced himself, and let the current carry the raft. By pushing the pole into the riverbed, he enjoyed floating in freedom. Tim didn't find it difficult to balance because the bamboo shafts were buoyant. He jumped off at the spot where Esther was and said with glee, "This is a blast!"

Instead of taking off for Port Antonio, Tim and Esther decided to take the day to encourage Nick and to talk with him about his new faith. They spent the day practicing riding on the water and the river bank watching the people float on by. They started to sing a song about floating in freedom, and after an afternoon of playing with words, a song emerged. Together Tim and Esther sang it for Nick. They sang:

In Freedom, We Ride
Dredging up the junk
Down in the dumps
Yet, the sun rises, and we see
That You lived and died so we can ride

No lead around our heads
Shackled to the past
Enslaved to death and wrath
The sun rises, and now we see

Jesus, You lived and died
So, in freedom we ride
This truth sets us free
The Spirit gives liberty

In freedom we ride
Above life's circumstance
We live by faith
With joy we dance

Jesus, You lived and died
So in freedom we ride
Jesus, You lived and died
So in freedom we ride
We have received power from on high
As Jesus and Peter walked on the water

Jesus, You lived and died
So in freedom we ride
Death, where is your sting?
We know that we have eternal life

Jesus, You lived and died
So in freedom we ride
Jesus, You lived and died
So in freedom we ride
"Mount Truth" girds us
Jesus, Your life saves us

Jesus, You lived and died
So in freedom we ride
Let freedom ring as we sing
Songs of victory, poems of praise

Raise the anchor, and set the sail
Chart the course and crest the waves
By faith we float above it all
Buoyed in your loving arms

Nick was inspired by the song and applauded their efforts. He could see his own story in the song and commented about it. Tim and Esther invested the evening talking with Nick about the glorious grace of God, a grace so great it can save pirates.

Their plan was to get up the next morning, and after breakfast, float down river to Port Antonio and continue their honeymoon. Tim and Esther were not looking forward to saying good-bye to Nick as they had just had a very special divine appointment with him.

10.

The Sinking of the *Satisfaction*

Nick was up with the chickens, and their clucking got him to go to the produce stands by the river. He purchased some cackle fruit from a boy who had fresh eggs in his basket. The boy couldn't believe how generous Nick was because he gave him a piece of a *piece of eight* for a bunch of eggs.

When Nick arrived back at the tent, Tim and Esther were excited to have a hot cooked meal and had started a fire for cooking. The smells of fried eggs in coconut oil with peppers were a delight. Esther served Nick and Tim some English tea and the men began to talk.

On the ship, Nick wasn't known for being much of a talker. He would tell you that he went along just to get along. But today he is feeling alive, rich, and free. God must have changed his life last night, because this morning he wants to get it all out. He is talking like a drunken parrot, but Nick is drunk in the Spirit. For some strange reason, he is compelled to unpack his entire life story.

Tim and Esther were encouraging and assured Nick that there was nothing in his previous life that God hadn't forgiven when Jesus died on the cross. But, regardless of this truth, Nick wanted to revisit his previous life of pirating. As he talked it out, he began to realize why he went the way of the pirate. He found acceptance on the ship; yet, it was clear that because of pirate pressure in him and all around him that he did things he wasn't proud of.

It was as if a light came on in his soul, and he began to sing these thoughts:

I'm Satisfied
Looking for things to fill my bucket
Shiny objects to hold in my hand
Steel to wield that says I am a man
Something that tells others
Stand back, "I got it"

Reality doesn't ease my pain
My earring is for my burial
The cutlass is to save my ass
"Skull and crossbones'" tats
Are low class

With wonder in his eyes, he talked about how stupid the pirate life was. And how they were not as alive, rich, and free as they made themselves out to be. He confessed that he was always afraid that he might say the wrong thing and get marooned on some shallow island by his shipmates as their commitment to him was about as shallow. Tim smiled, chuckled, cleared his throat, and began to sing:

My whole life
I've been chasing like a pirate
Until God's light sought me out
I basked in the sunshine of His love
Glory!
I've been found
I am accepted
I am loved
I am heaven bound

Stroking his beard and smiling, Nick said, "That is true, dammit. I've been chasing my whole lifelong. Who would have thought that God would seek me out?" Tim said, "Jesus is the Good Shepherd, who came looking for you. He found you, and He will make sure you make it home. Heaven is your new home." Nick said, "I am so unworthy." Tim said, "We all are, but He really does love you and came to get you out of hell and into heaven." Nick, with tears in his eyes and a lump in his throat, began to sing:

Shiver me timbers, matey
By faith
I don't have a hole in my soul
I have been made whole

The ocean couldn't fill
My empty soul
The plunder was never enough
Go on account
Live by adrenaline
Thinking the next cache
Would be the plum
Couldn't be more dumb
Raid and pillage, take, take, take
Always trying to make, make, make
Trained to chase
I was a head case
Doubled down and fake, fake, fake

I deserved to walk the plank
Drown in the drink
The abyss is filled
With dead men's dreams
It is Satan's scheme

Tim cheered this confession and added, "Our flesh, the bad part of us, like a pirate will always try to go on the make and take, take, take. But, we can walk in the Spirit now. You have a new life; the old man is crucified, and you are alive in Him. You are saved by Jesus' life. When He died, you died with Him. He rose from the dead. I tell you He is alive, and you are alive in Him." Then Tim sang:

I needed new eyes to be satisfied
Jesus spit in the dirt
Showed me my worth
Opened my eyes to see
I'm satisfied

Because He died
I'm satisfied
True treasure is won
My thirst is quenched
The hunger is gone
My chase is quashed
Because He died
I'm satisfied

I am no longer chasing
Pearls that are costly
O, Sink me, matey
I am His pearl of great cost

He made me for Himself
Knowing Him, I'm content
I am the apple of His eye
Now, I'm satisfied

Hallelujah, He died
Therefore I am justified
Now I am being sanctified
I will be glorified
All I can say is:
I'm satisfied

Nick was just shaking his head in joyful bliss, and he said, "That *Jolly Roger* would go up the flagpole, and we would chase. We would raid, pillage, plunder, and loot. When we got the treasure chest in the ship, we would divide it all. No one was ever really satisfied. The men would begin to fight each other over their pickings. Pirates are never satisfied." Tim said, "No such thing as a content pirate." While stroking his beard, Nick nodded his head affirmatively and said, "This is true." Then Tim sang:

He made me for Himself
This truth set me free
Shoot fire and boy howdy
It is hard to believe but
He is satisfied with me

How good it is!
I'm satisfied
Stand back
I got it!

Nick was so encouraged by these words, that he sang that stanza again with Tim:

He made me for Himself
This truth set me free
Shoot fire and boy howdy
It is hard to believe but
He is satisfied with me

How good it is!
I'm satisfied
Stand back
I got it!

Neither of these men were known for their singing voices, but they harmonized and sensed that God was well pleased with their fellowship. Esther applauded and smiled as she cleaned up the breakfast mess. Nick took the dirty skillet to the river to wash it out, and Tim began to pack up the tent. While washing the skillet, Nick had an epiphany and had to race back to Tim. He had a story on his heart that he had to get out.

They sat on a stoop they had made out of a log and enjoyed the crackling embers of the fire. Nick said, "I have to tell you a story, a story you won't believe, but it is true. You see, I sailed with Captain Morgan, and I was with him when his ass was in a corner. I tell you he didn't flinch; he knew exactly what to do. This is a story that reeks of pure pirate, and I am ashamed to tell it. But here goes:

"It was a miserable night. The ship was crewed by a bunch of miscreants, experienced sailing men, but that was a problem, too. They knew we were sailing into a trap, but there was nowhere else to go. Oh, there was a way out for the captain. We thought we were in this together, but the captain was a selfish *freebooter*."

Tim asked, "What do you mean? Not the Captain?" Nick answered, "He knew how to save his own skin; he was lots of thunder, but little rain. He wasn't insane; he knew how to smarten everyone up. He *scuppered* his crew. He didn't give a care. He was willing to make *shark bait* out of all of us. He wasn't going to *kiss the gunner's daughter, begad,* no. He was going to have us—his crew—do his dirty work and sacrifice our lives. *Arrrr!*

"We had been terrorizing the coast of Venezuela; we sailed into Lake Maracaibo with all 10 of our ships and attacked the little towns. This was the captain's method, and we had been been making a haul. Lots of gold! He would tie up the townspeople, and with a stick and a rope, he would have their heads squeezed until their brains almost popped out. Then they would tell us where their gold was buried. We would dig it up, pillage the place, and be on our way. But we had taken too much time, and the Spanish Armada was on to us. We could see their big ships in the distance. Their ships were large and slow. The stupid *swashbuckler* thought it would be easy to out run 'em, but it wasn't. We about got blown up by their cannons.

"We sailed on, you know, *yo-ho-ho.* But, we sailed into more Spanish ships stationed at the entrance to Lake Maracaibo. They were blocking the passageway out and had their cannons aimed at us. Quickly the captain ordered crew members to take some of the smaller boats and head to shore for ground warfare. Shoot fire, *matey*, he faked like he was joining us for a ground battle. He was known for that, but not this time. The captain knew the cannons would be turned on those men and they were. We had no idea what to do. There was going to be hell to pay, but the captain immediately ordered the ships to transfer the booty to his ship and then loaded his biggest ship with TNT and had a hundred men sail that ship straight away into their flagship.

"As ordered, the man hurled grappling hooks onto the Spanish flagship. With the ships tied together and all hell breaking loose in close combat, the TNT exploded. It was blood and guts. The cutlasses were stabbing and cutting—it was barbaric. Bodies were flying and the screams were demonic. It was an incredible fireworks show, but hundreds died. But one was saved. You know, the man in the red silk britches, he saved his own ass."

Tim said, "I could have guessed." Nick asked, "Tim, do you know the name of the ship Captain Morgan sacrificed to save his own skin?" Tim said, "No, what was it?" Nick was emphatic. "It was called the *Satisfaction*." Tim just shook his head, and Nick said, "Can you believe it?" Tim said, "Yes, I can. The stories are so wild that you hardly know what to believe." Nick said, "Hell, I was there and I can't get over it. He sank the *Satisfaction* to save his own hide." Tim asked, "How did you get out of there alive?" Nick said, "I kept my eye on the captain. When I saw that he wasn't joining the fight, I made a run for it. I commanded a small ship and later rejoined the *hornswaggler.*"

Tim asked, "How did the captain get out of that tight spot?" Nick disgustingly laughed, "You know the captain let the rising tide saunter his ship out into the current. He watched the fireworks, but he circumvented his remaining ships, and they sailed on." Tim said, "That is what pirates do. He made sure he had the booty, and he saved his own booty, if you know what I mean." Nick laughed, "I know what you mean."

Tim said, "The Christian life is not about saving our own skin. Jesus gave His life for us by dying on the cross." Tim took out his crumpled page of Scripture and was trying to show Nick a passage from Ephesians, Chapter 1 that shows how Jesus redeemed mankind by His sacrificial death. Nick looked at the page, but shook his head and said, "I can't read."

Tim put his arm around Nick's head and hugged his neck and said, "Nick, when you get back to Port Royal, look for Peter. And tell him you met Tim and Esther in Berrydale. Ask him to teach you God's Word. I know he will. When we get back after our honeymoon, we will teach you to read so you can digest God's Holy Word. His Word will build you up and lead you in God's everlasting ways. Besides, you will need some fellowship, too. You will find good friends with Peter."

Tim and Esther had a wonderful time with their new brother Nick. Nick mentioned that he was headed toward Port Royal to find Captain Morgan's plantation and see if the captain would employee him in his sugar cane operation. But, before they went their separate ways, Tim and Esther sang a song they had been working on, a song that speaks to some of the "I Am" names of Jesus. They sang:

In Him I Am Satisfied
In Him I am satisfied
He is the great I Am
I am satisfied in Him

Light of the world, You are
Like the stars, You dazzle our eyes
We are warmed and guided by Your light
You let us shine in the night

You are the Door to the sheepfold
Through You we enter in
You welcome us home
You shut the devil out

The smell of fresh bread thrills our souls
Your sacrifice makes us whole
Bread of life, savory, and sustaining
You make us strong

Nothing refreshes like cool water
Jesus, You are the living water
"Living water," drench us in your love
Quench us, refresh us

Faithful Shepherd, You lead us
You provide for us, we find rest
You protect us and meet our needs
Every need we have, You see

Jesus, You are the "true Vine," We bask in the Son
and grow
We abide and your sap flows
We drink the wine of Your love

Risen Lord, death couldn't hold you down
Those who look to You rise, too
You are the risen, living, Savior, King
Because You live, we ascend
In Him I am satisfied
He is the great "I Am"
I am satisfied in Him

As Light
You give sight

As the Door
You welcome us home

As bread
We savor You

As water
You satisfy our thirst

As the Vine
We abide in you

As our Shepherd
We follow You and find rest

As the Resurrection and the Life
We rise and live forever

You said, "I am the light of the world"
"I am the door" to the sheepfold
"I Am the 'Bread of life'"
"I Am the 'living water'"
"I Am the 'true Vine'"
"I Am the 'Good Shepherd'"
"I Am the 'Resurrection and the Life'"

In Him I am satisfied
He is the great "I Am"
I am satisfied in Him

You are the bright in light
You say welcome at the door
You are the yum of fresh bread
You are the "ah" of cool water

You are the sap that flows in our branches
You cause me to grow
We love to BASK
In the sunshine of Your love

You are alive from the dead
The risen and living Lord
You are the wow of life itself
We proclaim, in Him I am satisfied

Nick loved the song and applauded. Tim had the trio hold hands, and he prayed for God to lead them and to protect them in their travels. They all knew they had just experienced a heaven-ordained time that was a gift from God. Nick began his trek, and Tim and Esther boarded the *Adventurer*, the bamboo raft they had affectionately named. Esther sat in the middle on the tent pack with her bags at her feet. Tim joked that she was his Queen of Sheba as they sailed the Rio Grande. Tim was standing proud, his wife as his passenger, his hands on the long pole, and God as their Captain at the helm. This was a joy-filled day as they sailed in freedom and delighted in being in the current of God's grace, basking in the sunshine of God's love.

11.

Think Satisfaction/Be Satisfied

Riding the Rio Grande on top of the water on a bamboo raft couldn't have been grander. Esther enjoyed acting as the Queen of Sheba on her ship, and Tim felt fully alive, rich, and free as the captain of this version of the *Adventurer.*

The scenery was quintessential Jamaica, as it is the land of wood and water. The colorful flowers and the chirping birds seen in the trees, overhanging parts of the river, made for a delightful voyage to Port Antonio. Esther loved the ride, as she enjoyed this special honeymoon time with her husband. And Tim loved the ride because of how exhilarating and adventurous it was. They both were thrilled to have had a special day together on the river. As they were thanking God for making this day happen, Tim was also remembering Nick who snugged up the rope knots and helped him build this sturdy ship. It held together fine.

Port Antonio was a welcoming place. A young lad was eager to purchase the *Adventurer* from Tim, and he was happy to let her go. They had enough silver for a good dinner and some supplies. Tim and Esther didn't have far to go to the Blue Bay, but thought it was good not to push on, so they found a spot and set up their tent. Esther had time to stitch some flowers into the tallit and enjoyed relaxing with the river in view. Tim needed time to think. He reckoned that he really hasn't taken time in his whole life to really think. He knows that he has many things to think about.

While watching others on rafts come into Port Antonio, Tim is once again skipping rocks out onto the river and making a mental list of the things he needs to think about. For one, he can't get out of his head the image Nick told him about the sinking of the *Satisfaction*. He just knows that there is a lesson in this story for him personally. He also wants to take time to think about some of the lessons Papa Peter imparted in their counseling sessions. He knows that now he is ready to understand some of what Papa was trying to say.

As Tim is skipping rocks, he continues to think about his life. He keeps coming back to the moment he was *shanghaied* on the dock in London, knocked out, and awakened in pain on the *Adventurer*, as a conscript to pirates. As a slave on the ship, he was bound to a leaking vessel, a stinky crew, and subjected to all kinds of sinning. He also faced ridicule and various forms of rejection for his faith. He hasn't fully processed this experience, and the influence these rejections have had on his life.

As he throws the rocks harder and farther, he ponders the power rejection had on his life. He reckons that this "rejecting" experience was an evil plot against his sense of who he is. He knows that this was an evil attempt by Satan to get him to not "wear the CROWN," as Papa has taught him. It also got him to weigh too heavily the derisive things the savage crew members said about him. These things were said to try to sink him emotionally and spiritually.

Tim casts a larger rock out into the river, and, with the kerplunk, he sees the rings form around its landing spot. In this moment, he realizes that though he was *shanghaied* and severely rejected, God always accepted him. He sees that as a big ring in the water, and then he sees another ring of water and thinks about God providing Chase as a friend and a support. And the next water ring was a reminder of God's faithfulness to provide Papa Peter, the church community, and especially Esther. With thanksgiving in his heart, Tim knows that God has caused all things to work together for good in his life, because by God's grace, he loved God and was willing to submit to God's purpose for his life.

Standing on the side of the river, talking with God, shaking his head, and thinking about how God was faithful to bring him to this point in time—with a beautiful and godly wife—but how was he going to get his life in order and be a good husband?

Back in the tent, Esther has been stitching flowers into the tallit. She is thinking about the purpose of the tallit and knows that the husband and father of a Jewish family would cover his wife and children under the tallit and pray over them. She wishes Tim would take more spiritual leadership in their relationship, as she feels that he goes aloof from time to time and doesn't cover her as God wants him to. She reckons and remembers a verse from Psalm 91 that says God will take us under His wings. She thanks God for being her protector and for hiding her under His wing. She doesn't want to be a nag and gripe to Tim about his tendency to withdraw, as she fears he would only shrink back more if she were critical of him. So she offers up a simple prayer to God for her husband to become the spiritual leader God wants him to be.

Tim eventually makes his way back to the tent and finds Esther on the blanket with her sheets of Scripture, reading and crying. She isn't sobbing uncontrollably or anything, but Tim can tell she is a mess. He asks, "Esther, is there anything wrong?" Esther responds with tears on her cheeks, and a whimper, "I am just feeling sad." Tim said, "I am sorry, but why do you feel sad? We are having a good time, huh!" Esther says, "I got married to have a relationship with you, but you go and throw rocks in the river." Tim said, "I need to think about stuff." Esther said, "Try thinking with me!"

Tim, being uncomfortable with this conversation, tries to change the subject and asks, "What are you reading?" Esther wipes the tears off her face and says, "I am reading the Song of Songs, and it is a beautiful love story." Tim asked, "What is God saying to you?" Esther said, "They so loved being together that they were enthralled with each other." Tim said, "Show me what you like." Esther said, "No, it is personal." Tim said, "How can I know unless you show me?" Then moving close to Esther and sitting by her side, Esther reads from Solomon's Song, Chapter 2:

14

O my dove, in the clefts of the rock, In the secret *places* of the cliff, Let me see your face, Let me hear your voice; For your voice *is* sweet, And your face *is* lovely.

Tim clears his throat and says, "Let me see your face; let me hear your voice; for your voice is sweet, and your face is lovely." Esther says, "Oh, Tim, you are just making fun." Tim laughs and then asks, "Why is that verse so meaningful to you?" Esther says, "See how they love each other, how they long to be together. The lover wasn't off throwing rocks at the water." Tim is defensive and says, "I need some time to think about my life. I've done lots of stuff." Esther said, "Well, so have I. Let's think together." Tim had a bewildered look in his eyes, as if he had never pondered that idea before. He said, "That sounds like a good idea."

Esther then asked, "What 'stuff' have you been thinking about?" Tim said, *"Blimey,* I was thinking about the sinking of the *Satisfaction,* how Captain Morgan rammed his ship, the *Satisfaction,* into another ship and, with grappling hooks, had the two ships bound together. I am sure they both sank after the explosions went off." Esther asked, "Why does that story mean so much to you?" Tim said, "Can't you just see it? See the captain sailing off, while the ships sink and his crew drowns. Brutal, huh!"

Esther said, "Yes, and the captain was only about saving himself." Tim said, "That scares me. I know I can be selfish, too." Esther said, "When we look to Jesus, we become unselfish and then give ourselves to save others." Tim, wiping his brow with his sleeve, said, *"Aye,* that is true. He saved others." Esther said, "Let's look at a favorite Scripture and think about it together. She reached into Tim's britches and pulled out the well-worn pages. She read from Ephesians, Chapter 2:

8

For by grace you have been saved through faith, and that not of yourselves; *it is* the gift of God,

9

not of works, lest anyone should boast.

10

For we are His workmanship, created in Christ Jesus for good works, which God prepared beforehand that we should walk in them.

Tim said, "Well, that is about all we need to know, huh!" Esther laughed and said, "Yes, but do we really know it?" Tim said, "I know that grace is not anything we earn or deserve; it is just God loving us unconditionally and forgiving us." Esther said, "True, true, but so you see how God does it all? How He brings the grace and even the faith." Tim said, "What?" Esther said, "We have been saved by grace through faith." Tim said, "I hear you." Esther said, "See how God gives the grace, but also gives the faith for us to believe in Him, too?" Tim said, "No I haven't looked at it that way."

Esther said, "How did you look at it?" Tim said, "I just believed that Jesus did it all, you know, by dying on the cross." Esther said, "That is right, but that is only the beginning." Tim said, "Well, then, what else is there? There is nothing we can do to earn our salvation." Esther said, "I know, but after grace is applied in our lives, there is a lot of faith to grow into. And then there is that 'workmanship' part. As a result of our growth in faith, God has a work for us to do." Tim said, "I get it. There is more."

The couple went fishing together, and then made dinner together. They had a wonderful time by the river watching people ride the current into Port Antonio. For Esther, this was an immediate answer to a prayer. For Tim, he was taken aback, as he was just now beginning to see what a precious "helpmate" Esther was to him, as she had a beautiful mind and loved to think her way through the Scriptures. Her depth of knowledge didn't intimidate him; rather he was encouraged by how she enjoyed thinking through the Scriptures together.

As they were lying down and gazing at the stars, Tim asked, "Esther, were you named after Queen Esther in the Bible?" Esther said, "Yes, I was. Papa loved how she saved the nation of Israel by risking her life. He taught me that this Jewish woman was courageous and approached the king and touched the tip of the golden scepter and asked to speak to him. She then told him about the plight of the Jews and the evil plot against them. God used her, and Papa always taught me that this was God's call on my life." Tim said, "*Ahoy,* that is good!"

While lying there, Tim said, "That is a better picture than the sinking of the *Satisfaction!*" Esther said, "It sure is. Papa taught me about the CROWN as my identity in Christ, and the scepter being my authority as a believer." Tim asked, "I know about the crown, but what is this business about our authority?" Esther said, "This is very important. As a believer in Jesus, we have been given His name. We are His children, and just as He sits at the Father's right hand—the position of authority—we are positioned in Him and have the authority of His name and the power of His Word to grant us access to what we need in life and dominion over principalities and powers of darkness." Tim looked like a cannon just exploded and said, "Wow, Papa taught you that? Is that in the Bible?" Esther said, "It sure is, and this is why he named me Esther. He wanted me to wear the crown of identity and wield the Lord's scepter of authority."

Tim asked, "How did Jesus give us authority?" Esther responded, "Remember the Great Commission passage, where Jesus said in Matthew 28":

18

All authority has been given to Me in heaven and on earth.

19

Go therefore and make disciples of all the nations, baptizing them in the name of the Father and of the Son and of the Holy Spirit.

Tim said, "Yes, I know of that passage." Esther said, "Jesus has not only given us His life; He has imparted to us His authority, so we can make a difference and have His influence in this world." Tim said, "I have to think about that." Esther said, "Let's think about that together." Tim laughed and said, *"Ahoy!"*

As the couple retired for the evening after enjoying a delightful dinner of fish fried in coconut oil and vegetables, they just talked. Esther enjoyed sharing the story of the unlikely Queen Esther and her role in saving God's children from Haman's evil plot. Tim loved thinking about his newfound authority as a believer. He is contemplating the various ways it can be used in his life to experience more victory and freedom. As they basked in the glow of the dancing embers, the couple entered into the intimacy God reserves for a man and a woman who have entered into His covenant of marriage.

The next morning Tim was in the mood for bacon fried on the fire. He just loved scrambled eggs and bacon with fresh peppers. He went to a store in Port Antonio and purchased some bacon and brought it back to the tent. Esther was able to stoke the fledgling embers back into a fire, and they had a scrumptious breakfast before they took down their tent and hiked to the Blue Bay, where they planned to enjoy their honeymoon for a good while. While talking and working, they together penned a song, a song that tells the story of their last couple of days. They enjoyed singing it together.

Think Satisfaction; Be Satisfied
Cackle fruit, with peppers and bacon
Scones slathered in jam
Wash it down the hatch
With sweet tea, Yo-ho-ho!

Think Satisfaction
Be satisfied
Think Satisfaction
Be satisfied

Shanghaied, lost to the sea
Oh, sink me, a slave to the crew
Conscripted and mistreated
Miscreant's gangway!

Think satisfaction
Be satisfied
Think satisfaction
Be satisfied

Think of the Father and be loved
Think of the Son and be known
Think of the Spirit and be raised
Think of heaven and be hopeful
Think of friends and be happy
Think of holding her hand and be moved

Think satisfaction
Be satisfied
Think satisfaction
Be satisfied

The world, the flesh, and the devil
Try to take me down
In the abyss to drown
Yet buoyed by God's presence

Think satisfaction
Be satisfied
Think satisfaction
Be satisfied

Tempted to shrink back
Wallow in shame
I've learned to say His name
His name, "Jehovah Saves"'
Think satisfaction
Be satisfied
Think satisfaction
Be satisfied

Think of purpose
Be rewarded
Think of the cross
Be valued
Think love
Be secure
Think faith
Be filled

Butterflies, hummingbirds
Beautiful trees and flowers
And refreshing waves of grace
Embrace my soul and I soar

Think satisfaction
Be satisfied
Think satisfaction
Be satisfied

He is an
Ocean of delight
I am precious in His sight

Smell the bread?
Taste the jam?
See the flowers?
Hear the birds sing?
Feel the grass and hold a hand?
There is nothing to dread!

Think satisfaction
Be satisfied
Think satisfaction
Be satisfied

Think faith
Be filled
Think truth
Be free
Think joy
Be strong
Think peace
And belong

Rainbows and stars
Moon and sun, too
Bask in His light
Experience delight

Think satisfaction
Be satisfied
Think satisfaction
Be satisfied

They really liked this song, because it told the story of their spiritual experience. And it applied the lesson of their authority that Jesus the King has given to them.

12.

Living Satisfied in the River of Pleasure

im and Esther didn't hear the eruptions, as they were miles away, but they did see the plumes and gushes into the clouds. They are now receiving black carbon and soot onto their tent. Concerned about breathing this charred debris into their lungs, they use the tallit as a cover and a filter, so they don't gag and cough. There is nowhere to run, as the whole island is being blanketed by this storm of soot.

They slept peacefully inside their tent made of a sail from the *Adventurer* and under the tallit. Just like being under the eagle's wing, protected near to the heart of God and sheltered by His embrace, they were encouraged.

The next morning, the spewing of ash and soot was beginning to subside. With their mouths and noses covered with their blouses, they make their way back to the Port Antonio point of the beach and discover that the Soufrière Hills volcano on the island of Montserrat had blown her top, and the breeze was blowing the dark cloud their way. Tim and Esther took the day to think about the volcano and their lives in perspective.

They stayed the day in their tent under the fabric of the sail and the colorful tallit, and they talked. Tim reasoned that Jamaica was a colorful island of wood and water and lush soil because the volcanic activity in the region made for a productive land. Esther thought that God had a very creative means of making and remaking the earth by means of volcanic flares.

Tim made a personal application of this experience from nature, as he reasoned that there were times that he "blew his top," too. He admitted that he has had an anger problem, and like the volcano, he had been known to erupt with angry outbursts. He said, "I need for God to tame my volcano." Esther tried not to laugh, but chuckled and said, "Tim, I don't see you as an angry volcano. I see you as a self-controlled man of God." Tim said, "I mask my feelings well. You know when I go and throw rocks, often it is just a way to spew my anger without hurting you. I have been afraid that I could hurt you with an angry outburst."

Esther said, "You are serious, aren't you?" Tim said, "Yes, I am. You know how pirates pull their *boucan* and start flailing away at the drop of a hat, all because they have the caldron inside their evil hearts boiling up inside like a teapot." Esther said, "That is a great word picture; you can paint with words." Tim smiled and said, "Thanks, but that darn volcano really brought a dark cloud, and it can be suffocating." Esther said, "Tim, I trust in God, and I trust you, too. I am glad that we are now talking about everything; I think as we talk together and pray together, your angry volcano will be tamed." Tim said, "I hope so. I love you, and I don't want to hurt you or anyone else."

In the days to come, the skies cleared, and the couple suffered no ill affects from the dark cloud. After a refreshing rain, it was as if the volcano had never blown up. They had shaken out their tent, and the tallit and everything seemed new again. The flowers were popping with brilliant color, and the turquoise blue water in the bay was inviting, so Tim and Esther enjoyed swimming, playing, and diving in the bay. They enjoyed many days of just relaxing and luxuriating in this paradise. Together they loved diving under the water and following the colorful and artistically designed fish. They could hardly believe how creative God had been to make so many beautiful fish with colors, shapes, and designs beyond imagination.

They took much time to talk together, and their favorite topic was the "grace of God." They had memorized a passage from Ephesians, Chapter 2, which reads:

8

For by grace you have been saved through faith, and that not of yourselves; *it is* the gift of God,

9

not of works, lest anyone should boast.

10

For we are His workmanship, created in Christ Jesus for good works, which God prepared beforehand that we should walk in them.

The couple reckoned that their honeymoon at this beautiful Blue Bay was an example of God's grace. They both knew that they didn't deserve to be in a beautiful place like this; that they didn't deserve to have the time like this; that they didn't do anything to earn the fish or the fruit God had provided right in their sight. They were starting to get ahold of this idea of grace, but realized that God's grace was far greater and richer than they could ever imagine, but they sure enjoyed talking about it.

Esther broached the subject of their future and asked, "Tim, we, in response to God's grace, are His workmanship created for good works. So, what are we going to do in the future?" Tim said, "I know that because of grace we don't 'have to' do anything, but I think we will want to go back to Port Royal and serve the community there and reach out to the sailing men and even the women in the sex trade." Esther swooned and said, "That is exactly what I want to do, too. I remember hearing about how my mother would take fruit and garden vegetables to the dock to sell, but also to minister to the people. Maybe we can have a farm and do the same? I just want to share this wonderful grace of God as expressed in the glorious Gospel with a lost and dying world." Tim said, "You have a good way with words."

Together they hugged, kissed, and went for a long walk up and down the Blue Bay, while talking about their future ministry plans. Tim was amazed at how excited Esther got about him and their future just by talking together. By God's grace, they came to understand that they were now living satisfied in the river of pleasure. Both were amazed to discover that God is not only a lover of pleasure, He is the Creator of pleasure, and He delights to see His children experience the pleasures He has designed for them. In His presence are pleasures forevermore.

Together they sat down and thought about some of the ways God is a lover and Creator of pleasure. Tim said, "God has given us tea—what a gift!" Esther laughed and said, "He has given us chocolate. Oh, how sweet!" Tim said, "True, true, and how we love it, but He also made the sugar cane." Esther said, "And look at the water and the trees with the fruit." Tim said, "If God didn't love us, we would just have hot sand and starve." Esther said, "I remember Psalm 16, where it says, 'At Your right hand are pleasures forevermore'." Tim thought for a while and said, "You know who is seated at His right hand?" Esther smiled and said, "Wow, yes, it is Jesus, and through Jesus and His grace, we have pleasure forevermore." Tim was drop-jawed amazed. It was like he was *harpooned* with a thought. He said, "We are in Christ; therefore, we are at the right hand of the Father with Him; we get His pleasures forevermore!" Esther said, "Wow! That is a great insight!"

They took some time and discussed how the ministry of the Holy Spirit gave them pleasure and how the Word of God was written for our pleasure. And then they remembered family, friends, and the fellowship back home that gave them so much pleasure. Together they were surprised to discover that God is a lover of pleasure and put together these thoughts. They reckoned that just about everything God has done in one way or another was for His own pleasure, and in some way, a way to bring His children into His pleasure. Esther said, "I have read about heaven, and it is packed full of pleasure for God's children." Tim said, "It is good to think together. *Shiver me timbers,* I didn't know that we were made to experience pleasure before this. And I certainly didn't know that God is a lover of pleasure." Esther said, "He is not the religious taskmaster that some people make Him out to be." Tim just nodded his head in agreement.

The couple then took some time to think together and write a poem to try and capture these inspiring thoughts. After a siesta time of thinking out loud, they came up with this poem and sang it back and forth.

Living Satisfied in the River of Pleasure

Living satisfied in the river of pleasure
Flowing freely in the current of His grace
Basking radiantly in the sunshine of His love
I am content to enjoy Him and thus fulfill my purpose

Satisfied in relationship with God
Nothing is held against us
He fulfills our desires and meets our needs
Indeed, He is our desire

It is a pleasure to treasure His presence
This is the essence of life and purpose
His love is continuously poured into our lives
Praise Him for His glorious grace

Praise Him for His glorious grace
With thanksgiving, we bask in His Son
His glory shows on our faces
His kindness has given life, freedom, and riches

An extravagant purchase with the blood
The ultimate victory has been won
We bask in Him and fulfill His plan
Forever we proclaim Jesus the "Son" is God

Rays of light shining bright
We are precious in His sight
Light with joy, filled with hope

Beaming, gleaming, and upbeat
As His glory shines in us

Radiant life, sincere desire
Waiting for the rapture
Living satisfied in the river of pleasure

Tim had assembled a pile of bamboo and
made himself a raft. He remembered the knots Nick

tied and was able to make a vessel just to play on and float around in the bay. He had been enjoying God in a personal way and enjoying his wife on this honeymoon. He was happy with God and his wife and couldn't ask for more. To say he was satisfied would be an understatement. He had been learning to delight in God and enjoy his wife. This was life at its best.

After an exhilarating swim in the bay, chasing some colorful fish diving and following them under the water, Tim is basking in the sunshine of God's love and lofting on the raft. Tim hears giggles and looks over his shoulder and sees young women running toward the bay. His bay is being invaded. Sensing that he wasn't noticed, he quietly falls off of the raft and into the bay. Able to stand in the shallow, he hides his head behind the raft and watches these women undress and go for a swim. He is mesmerized by their bodies and can't take his eyes off them. He stays hidden and can hardly turn his head from them. He looks to the tent to see if Esther is looking. He knows that he should flee the situation, but his flesh craves the stimuli of these bathing beauties.

Esther was in the tent, content to stitch some flowers into the tallit and to stay out of the sun, but when Tim finally made it back to the tent, she could tell that something was wrong with Tim. He wasn't talking. He was stonewalling again, and she asked,

"Tim, what is the matter?" Tim denied that anything was wrong. But Esther insisted. After a while of uncomfortable silence, Tim confessed, "Some women came to the water, undressed, and began to swim, and I watched them. I don't understand why I even wanted to observe them, but I did it. I am sorry; I am sad, and I am ashamed." Esther paused and then said, "Tim this sounds like a problem that is common to man, Jesus has already forgiven you. I forgive you. Why don't you forgive yourself, too?"

Tim couldn't believe her grace, her understanding, and patience and said, "You don't understand. I looked at them." Esther said, "I know. I wish you wouldn't have, but you are a man. I also know that it is the mercy of God that inspires us to really change, **not** the law! Do you want victory in your life?" Tim said, "Yes, I want victory, but I have failed again." Esther said, "This **is** a victory. You came to me, and we talked about it. Maybe next time, you can be like Joseph and flee the temptation. You and I know that God is faithful to provide ways of escape."

Tim, with his head in his hands, slowly lifts up his head, looks at Esther, smiles, and thanks her for her grace and understanding and said, "Yes, I believe that. I will just run to you and to God." Esther reached out to Tim and held him close to her heart. After a good long embrace, Tim began to feel strong again. Esther began to sing:

Lord Make Me a Channel

Lord make me a channel of your peace;
Where there is hatred, let me sow peace
Where there is injury, pardon
Where there is doubt, faith
Where there is darkness, light

Where there is sadness, joy
O, Divine Master, grant that I may not so much
Seek to be consoled, as to console
To be understood, as to understand
To be loved, as to love

For it is in giving that we receive
It is in pardoning, that we are pardoned
And it is in dying
That we are born again to eternal life
—Saint Francis of Assisi

Tim was smiling radiantly and applauding Esther, singing her favorite song. But, mostly Tim was amazed to discover in his soul that real satisfaction was intimately related to one's ability to receive grace, and, in turn, release grace. Esther showed him a mighty river of grace. Together they sat down and meditated on the crumpled page of Scripture Tim had faithfully kept in his britches. They read Ephesians 1:3–6:

3

Blessed *be* the God and Father of our Lord Jesus Christ, who has blessed us with every spiritual blessing in the heavenly *places* in Christ,

4

just as He chose us in Him before the foundation of the world, that we should be holy and without blame before Him in love,

5

having predestined us to adoption as sons by Jesus Christ to Himself, according to the good pleasure of His will,

6

to the praise of the glory of His grace, by which He made us accepted in the Beloved.

Esther really enjoyed this passage and said, "Now we know where God gets His pleasure." Tim asked, "Where?" Pointing to the print, Esther said, "Seeing us become part of His family is where God gets His pleasure." Tim said, "I see it and growing in grace, too!" Esther said, "Yes, that is how to live satisfied in the river of pleasure."

As they sat there basking in the sunshine of God's love, they decided to walk over to the trees and see if they could gather some mangoes and avocados for a meal. While looking up in the branches, Tim was intrigued to look at a vine that was trying to grow up the tree, but as he looked down, he noticed its large leaves reaching out toward the sun. But, to his delight, he found a large green watermelon begging for his pleasure.

Tim picked it and showed it off to Esther, and then, with great delight, they took it to their table. With his ax, he sliced it into pieces. They enjoyed a wonderful meal, but there was Tim taking big bites of this lusciousness and spitting seeds all over the place. He was bragging at how good a "spitter" of seeds he was and challenged Esther to spit with him. To his surprise, Esther couldn't spit. All she would do was blubber, and seeds would dribble off of her lip. He tried hard not to laugh, but Esther said, "I can sing, but I can't spit." Then Tim laughed. Esther said, "Spitting is not something I aspire to."

Tim couldn't get over how sweet and delicious the watermelon was. Always the daughter of her father, she said, "Did you see how the watermelon vine was growing? How the leaves on the vine were reaching out and basking in the sunshine?" Tim said, "Yes, I saw that." Esther opined, "The leaves on the vine soaked in the sunshine, and the sap flowed in the vine and filled the watermelon with goodness." Tim laughed and said, "What a picture. That is really how we are to be, huh!" Esther smiled and said, "Papa would be proud. He would say, 'Let the SAP flow,' and he meant the Spirit and the anointing are released as we praise God."

Tim clapped his hands and said, "That is good, Esther. But, did you notice the soil it was growing in?" Esther said, "I didn't." Tim said, "You know the ash from the volcanoes made for good soil for the watermelon to grow." Esther said, "I think the Lord above has given us some good soil, too. It is fun to grow in Christ with you. I love thinking about God's ways with you." Tim felt happy, happy to be flowing in grace, truly satisfied in the river of pleasure.

Tim and Esther enjoyed their honeymoon at the Blue Bay in the fall of 1691 and would return home to serve the community of Port Royal and her many visitors. They are committed to dispensing the marvelous and rich grace of God and delight in seeing the glorious Gospel make people alive, rich, and free.

A View From the Crow's-Nest

Questions for deeper personal study or small group discussions

Chapter 1: Bask Your Way to Satisfaction

From the Pirate Speak list of words, pick three of the words and explain why a pirate is never satisfied. Explain what it means to be satisfied. How does "Basking" in the sun help for satisfaction? How does basking in the "Son" help one discover satisfaction? How do Peter's BASK motions help him experience satisfaction. (Try the hand movements and work through each letter in BASK.)

Chapter 2: God Is the Ocean of Delight

Why do some people think of God as a disgruntled school principal? Do you see God as an "ocean of delight?" Why? Or why not? As Tim gets ready to marry Esther, why is it important for him to know that he has satisfaction in God first? Why would Esther want Tim to have satisfaction in God before they marry? Why would most people rather "kiss the gunner's daughter" than be truly honest about their soul? Do you think this is true? Why? Or why not? How is God the ocean of delight? How can you enjoy Him more? What name for God inspires you to enjoy Him more? Why?

Chapter 3: Wedding Preparations

Why is it important to have a wedding ceremony? What does commitment have to do with satisfaction in marriage? How does Papa's (Lily's) wedding ring impart blessing? In your opinion, what is a Christian marriage? How does Papa compare wedding preparations to gardening? Which illustration from gardening means the most to you? Why? From Ephesians 5:15–33, what are some of the responsibilities for the man in marriage? For the woman?

Chapter 4: White Waterfall Wedding

Papa was confident that every provision had been made for Tim and Esther to be satisfied in marriage. What are some of those provisions? Why do they matter? Tim was fearful that he had lost his innocence because of his experiences on the *Adventurer*. How will God's love push fear out of his life? How is grace the great equalizer when it comes to reconciling all the differences each person brings to a marriage? Both Tim and Esther had different expectations and desires for their marriage. How can they have peace when their expectations and motivations are messed up? Chase gave the couple a tallit, a Jewish prayer shawl. How does this symbol express God's covering over us? How does it show the man's role in covering his wife and children? (Look at Psalm 91.) How did getting married God's way make for satisfaction on their wedding night?

Chapter 5: The Tallit and the Tent

The wedding night presented many surprises to the couple. How was Esther surprised? How was Tim surprised? Why is it a beautiful thing to have these surprises? How do the differences between male and female make sexuality in marriage excellent? Why is innocence so important to realize in Christian marriage? Esther struggled with inadequacy. What did Tim struggle with? How could they have helped each other better with their feelings of inadequacy? According to James 1:2–3 and Romans 5:2–5, how can struggle make a person and a marriage better? How did the sensuality in the Song of Solomon blow Tim away?

Chapter 6: Coconuts, Chocolates, and Limes

Why is it important for Esther to know that Tim cherishes her as a person and not just for her sexuality? By being away on a honeymoon and not having Christian community to lean on, how are they being strengthened? Weakened? The couple struggles with communication. Why is it important to learn how to share feelings and opinions in marriage? Why did Tim clam up and not share enough? How did this make it tough on Esther? How did they move from intimacy to isolation? Then back to intimacy? What do coconuts, chocolates, and limes show us about God? About His love for pleasure? Why would He give us these delicacies? Tim learned a lesson when he overly squeezed a lime. In your opinion, what was the lesson he was to learn?

Chapter 7: Shanghaied Again

How does experiencing God in nature revive the soul? Your soul? What did it take for Tim and Esther to feel like the richest people in the world? What will it take for you to feel rich? Esther is put off by Tim's overture for sex. Why is this so off-putting for Esther? Tim tends to move toward isolation when embarrassed. How does this bonehead action affect their intimacy? Why? Tim reflects again on his past rejections. Why is the past backward direction a wrong direction for our minds to go? What all does he really need to know from his past? Why are rejections so painful? Why do rejections enflame our flesh (the little pirate)? Why does Satan play on our past? How can he be defeated? How was he defeated? Esther begins to think that all men are "pirate-like." What direction should she be taking her thoughts instead? From the song "Shanghaied Again," what are your favorite lyrics? Why?

Chapter 8: Boa and Butterflies

Tim had withdrawn from Esther emotionally— Esther is tempted to react with performance-based love. What is performance-based love? Why is this contrary to grace? Why does it backfire in marriage? Tim apologized for "stonewalling." What is stonewalling? Why is this harmful to a relationship? What does Esther mean by the "dutty tough?" What is the spiritual application here?

In the song "I Am a Man," Tim begins to own up to his identity as a man and assume his responsibilities. What is his true identity? What are his responsibilities? (What has wearing the CROWN got to do with it?) How did words shanghai Tim? Esther? You? How did the boa constrictor scare Esther? How did she relate this scare to her own life? How does Tim's silence shanghai Esther? How does the process from worm to butterfly encourage the couple? You? How can we "crush" the serpent? Why is it important to know that you have authority over evil when it comes to your relationships?

Chapter 9: Riding in Freedom

How is marriage by design going to bring the best out of Tim? Esther? How does it bring out the worst? Why? (What is God's idea here?) How is riding on a bamboo raft like walking in the Spirit? Nick "Neck-beard" meets up with Tim and Esther. Why do people often refer to people by their physical characteristics? Why is this harmful? How can we do better? In you opinion, why did Tim name their raft the *Adventurer*? Tim shares the gospel with Nick. What is the gospel? Why does the gospel mean "good news?" What does Nick need to do to have a real relationship with God? Why is it difficult for Nick to accept God's grace? For you? How does Tim help Nick understand and receive God's grace? Why was Esther so pleased to hear her husband share the good news with Nick? What does evangelism do for you? (See Philemon v. 6.)

Chapter 10: The Sinking of the *Satisfaction*

How do you know that Nick got saved? What does his generosity have to do with it? If anything? In the song "I'm Satisfied," what is the main message? What lyrics mean the most to you? Why? Nick tells the story of Captain Morgan sinking his flagship the *Satisfaction*. Why did the captain do this? How do we often sink our own satisfaction? Intentionally?

Unintentionally? What do you do to sink your own satisfaction in life? How does Captain Morgan the pirate show us scurvy pirate flesh? What, in your opinion, were his flesh tendencies? What are your favorite names for Jesus found in the song "In Him I Am Satisfied?" What is the main message of this song? What does it take to be satisfied in this life? Why did Esther feel like a queen riding the Rio on the *Adventurer*? How were they basking in the sunshine of God's love? Why is basking the key to satisfaction? (Review the hand motions.)

Chapter 11: Think Satisfaction/Be Satisfied

As Tim skips rocks in Port Antonio, what is he thinking about? Why are our thoughts so important? Why is it so important to think "satisfaction?" What power did rejection have in Tim's life? Your life? Why does Esther demand that Tim think with her? What does the Bible mean when it says "let me see your face" (Song of Solomon)? How does the song "Think Satisfaction/Be Satisfied help you to experience satisfaction in your life? Is experiencing satisfaction that simple that you can think your way to satisfaction? Have you seriously tried to do it?

Chapter 12: Living Satisfied in the River of Pleasure

How did the tallit cover the couple during the volcanic eruptions? How does God's love cover us? How did the volcano help Tim reckon with his anger problem? How has the couple begun to communicate better? (Examples) What does this improvement mean to Esther? To Tim? How has this helped them experience satisfaction? How has Ephesians 2:8–10 been applied to their lives? How has Esther shown grace to Tim when he failed? How has Tim demonstrated grace to Esther? How doe vision for their future help the couple? Why is vision so important to Esther? To Tim? How does God give us a glorious future?

Why does Satan always want you to live in the past? How did the watermelon bring happiness to the couple? What caused the watermelon to grow? What were Tim's observations? What do you need to grow? How will you bask in the sunshine of God's love for you today? Tomorrow? Forever? What does the Peter mean by "let the SAP flow?"

Songs, Poems, and Authors
BASK Satisfaction

Chapter One:

"All Creatures of Our God and King," by Saint Francis of Assisi, circa 1225

"Glisten for Your Glory," by Sid and Karen Huston, 2019

Chapter Two:

"Like Diamonds the Brilliance," by Sid Huston, 2019

Chapter Three:

"The Power of an Endless Life," by Sid Huston, 2019

Chapter Four:

"Every Provision," by Sid Huston, 2019

Chapter Five:

"Beloved," by Sid Huston, 2019

Chapter Seven:

"Shanghaied Again," by Sid Huston, 2019

Chapter Eight:

"I Am a Man," by Sid Huston, 2019

"Crushed It," by Sid Huston, 2019

Chapter Nine:

"In Freedom We Ride," by Sid Huston, 2019

Chapter Ten:

"I'm Satisfied," by Sid Huston, 2019

"In Him I'm Satisfied," by Sid Huston, 2019

Chapter Eleven:

"Think Satisfaction; Be Satisfied," by Sid Huston, 2019

Chapter Twelve:

"Living Satisfied in the River of Pleasure," by Sid Huston, 2019

"Lord Make Me a Channel," by Saint Francis of Assisi, circa 1224

Scripture Index
BASK Satisfaction

Bible References Include:

Chapter One: Bask Your Way to Satisfaction

Matthew 5:16

1 John 1:5–7

Chapter Two: God Is the Ocean of Delight

Psalm 37:4–5

Psalm 103:5

Psalm 34:3

Chapter Three: Wedding Preparations

Ephesians 5:15–33

Chapter Four: White Waterfall Wedding

Song of Songs

Psalm 91

Ephesians 5:25–27

Chapter Five: The Tallit and the Tent

Song of Solomon 1:2–6

Song of Solomon 2:4–5

About Sid Huston

Sid grew up in Grand Island, Nebraska. He was a typical kid, loved the Huskers football team, and dreamed of playing professional basketball. As a student, he was a classic underachiever and had four sharp siblings right behind him, "spurring" him on. After high school graduation, he attended a Christian sports camp where he was introduced to a personal relationship with Jesus.

This relationship with Jesus Christ gave the trajectory of Sid's life a dramatic shift upward. Though he still loved sports, he got involved in various Christian ministries and was thrilled by experiencing lives transformed for the better upon hearing the gospel. He pledged himself to gospel ministry, and through the influence of godly friends, he became involved in spiritual leadership, seminary, and the local church. He has always been involved is some sort of sports ministry through playing, coaching, or radio.

He married Karen, who outclassed him by a mile. Together they have two married children and two grandsons. They have enjoyed encouraging each other in life and various ministry adventures. By God's grace, Sid has lived a faithful and fruitful life of faith. He has helped many people through personal evangelism, preaching, counseling, coaching and speaking.

The BASK series of books has put fresh wind in his sails and helped him flow in the current of God's grace. His books—written, electronic, and audio—are helping people discover life and freedom by appropriating the power of a true identity.

Sid lives to "wear the CROWN" and helps others wear the CROWN, too. He explains CROWN as Christ, Righteousness, Order, Worship, and Nobility. He draws this inspiration from Isaiah 61:1–3:

1

The Spirit of the Sovereign LORD is on me, Because
the LORD has anointed me to proclaim good news
to the poor. He has sent me to bind up the broken-
hearted, to proclaim freedom for the captives and
release from darkness for the prisoners,

2

to proclaim the year of the LORD's favor and the day of vengeance of our God, to comfort all who mourn,

3

and provide for those who grieve in Zion—to bestow on them a crown of beauty instead of ashes, the oil of joy instead of mourning, and a garment of praise instead of a spirit of despair. They will be called oaks of righteousness, a planting of the LORD for the display of His splendor.

www.ingramcontent.com/pod-product-compliance
Lightning Source LLC
Chambersburg PA
CBHW022151260626
47155CB00017B/1773